Blind Date Bet

Blind Date Bet

A Man's Best Friend Romance

Nicole Flockton

TULE
PUBLISHING

ISBN: 978-1-949707-45-8

Dedication

To Shey and Shawn

Chapter One

AN ALARM BLARED, loud and obnoxious, the second Isabella Knowles walked out of the clothes shop. She froze, glanced over her shoulder, and saw the store assistant marching toward her.

What the hell?

Reaching into her handbag, she rummaged for the receipt. No way was she going to be accused of stealing when she'd paid for the items in the bag fair and square.

Before the girl could reach her, movement outside of the shop registered with her. People were dashing down the mall, not in an *I need the bathroom* kind of way but more in the *get me the hell out of here* way.

"Ma'am." The assistant tapped her on the shoulder. "Can you please move? I need to secure the shop."

"What's going on?" Isabella asked. The alarm suddenly stopped its screeching.

"Attention, shoppers," a disembodied voice crackled around the store, echoing in the mall. "Due to unforeseen circumstances, we are evacuating the mall. Shoppers, please make your way to the closest exit in an orderly fashion.

Thank you."

The siren fired up again, and Isabella choked back a laugh and muttered, "I'll make my way to the nearest exit in an orderly fashion. Can't guarantee everyone else will."

"Ma'am, you heard the announcement, can you please leave the shop?" The assistant's voice had gone from semi-polite to downright rude.

"Sure, but will you girls be okay getting out?" They'd done plenty of fire drills at school; a cool head made things a lot easier for everyone. Others didn't feel this way so much, as evidenced by the stampede in front of the shop.

"Yes, ma'am. Now *leave.*"

Isabella blew out a long breath and shrugged. Fine, they didn't need her help. Making sure to pop her car keys into her pocket before exiting the store, Isabella made her way out into the crowd and was immediately swept up in the wave of people.

She weaved her way through the horde to get to the side of the rush where it wasn't so chaotic and she didn't fear getting stomped on.

At the nearest fire escape, a swarm of people all vied to get through the door first. There was a reason why they taught the kids to leave the classroom and schools in a line—less chance of a bottleneck at the exits.

Looking around, she noticed that the crowds were thinning; at least in the parking lot there would be plenty of room for people to spread out. The siren still blared, and if she strained her ears, she was sure she could make out the faint tones of the approaching first responders.

Or wait… no, that sounded like a child crying.

Forgetting everything drummed into her during evacuation training, Isabella spun around and worked her way through the mass of bodies. To her left, she noticed a little boy crying; he looked like one of the second graders from the school where she taught.

"Where the heck are his parents?" she murmured under her breath as she made her way toward him.

"Ma'am, you're going in the wrong direction."

Even though everything in her was screaming to get to the little boy, she swiveled to face the person who'd stopped her progress.

"I'm a school teacher, and I see one of my students. He's alone and I need to get him."

Standing in front of her was a fine specimen of a man. The cliched phrase *tall, dark, and handsome* sprang to mind, but the description suited him. His rugged appearance matched his deep voice.

"This child isn't your responsibility. The authorities will deal with him. You need to be concerned for your own safety."

Isabella ran her gaze over him, taking in the faded denim jeans he was wearing, the tight T-shirt that molded his broad shoulders and hugged his chest. He definitely wasn't a store security guard or even a first responder, so she didn't really need to follow his instructions. If he was a police officer directing her out, she'd listen. But the guy was a complete stranger. Where did he get off telling her what she could and couldn't do?

"Actually, as someone who is in charge of the child's education, yes, he is my responsibility. Now if you'll excuse me, he's run off and I need to find him."

She gripped her shopping bags tighter in preparation to brush past him, but he stepped in front of her, blocking her way. "Are you always this stubborn, or is it just my lucky day that you're being obstinate?" He practically growled at her.

Isabella sucked in a breath. "I don't know who you are, but you don't get to talk to me that way. Now please *move* so I can make sure the little boy is okay."

"Ma'am, if you go after the boy, you're only making things more difficult for the men and women trained in these circumstances. For your safety, and the safety of others, I suggest you turn around and exit the mall." He crossed his arms over his broad chest, giving her the impression of a brick wall.

Who is this guy?

The urge to argue more built inside of her. She'd spent the last few years answering to no one but herself. Unfortunately, she had to admit this stranger was correct. Rationally, it was stupid to go after the boy she'd caught only a glimpse of. All the training she'd completed reiterated not to put yourself in danger.

"Fine." Without waiting to see his self-satisfied smile, Isabella whirled around, her short skirt floating around her legs in a swish.

By the time she reached the exit, there was no crowd and she made her escape. Cars streamed out of the parking lot. Cars and trucks with flashing lights flooded in. A shiver rippled down her spine. Whatever was going on was serious, and the guy who'd demanded she leave had probably done her a favor.

But no way was she going to admit that to him if she ever saw him again, which was never going to happen.

Chapter Two

E THAN NEEDED HIS head examined.

There was no other explanation as to why he was standing in front of a coffee shop, under the simmering Texas summer sun, wearing a bright red fedora. Never, on his grandfather's grave would he partake in a slam-dunk shots contest with his buddy, Lincoln Forrest, who was in the army, ever again.

Sober, he never would've agreed to a blind date, not after the time Linc had talked him into meeting Kathy Birdland. Talk about disaster from the moment she opened her mouth. He shuddered now remembering the high-pitched twang she emitted and the tobacco-stained teeth that had greeted him when she smiled. He was surprised he hadn't landed in the *Guinness Book of World Records* under the shortest date category. Later, he'd found out the real Kathy Birdland had chickened out and paid some random woman fifty bucks to go on the date with him.

And yet, here he waited, on the sidewalk in downtown San Antonio, about to repeat the same mistake.

What he needed to do was swear off tequila shots.

Tequila had led him to wearing a red fedora so school teacher Isabella Knowles would recognize him. He should've gone with the more obvious I'm-holding-a-red-rose-because-I'm-a-sucker-on-a-blind-date look. As it was, people were glancing warily at him as they passed, no doubt wondering if he was a pimp or a wannabe drug dealer. Ethan glanced at his watch again. Still another five minutes until his supposed date was due to turn up.

Linc had assured Ethan Isabella was hot. As in H-O-T, hot. She didn't wear glasses. Wasn't a spinster with fifty cats. Had all her teeth, which weren't stained yellow. Didn't need to dye the gray out of her hair.

He automatically reached down to scratch the back of Sam's head, but he met fresh air. Of course, his dog wasn't on this date. He'd left Sam at the base to enjoy her weekend. Although having his K-9 partner standing beside him would distract him from waiting to see if Isabella resembled the bride of Chucky or a Victoria Secret's runway angel.

"Umm, I know this is going to sound really weird, but are you Ethan Masters?"

Holy smokes, her voice. Sexy, sultry like a good malt whiskey sliding down his throat. He only hoped her looks matched the voice. What would that voice sound like whispering in his ear when they were in the throes of passion?

Whoa, slow down, airman.

He turned slowly, keeping his eyes down. The first thing

he saw were bright purple toenails with white flowers painted on the big toes. Straps of gold crisscrossed the tops of her feet.

A delicate gold chain of tiny hearts encircled one slender ankle. He failed in not imagining those tanned legs wrapped around his waist. The black fabric of her skirt swirled just above her knees and a red shirt was tucked into it.

The V-neck of her top displayed a hint of cleavage, enough to entice but not enough to be tasteless. Finally, he lifted his gaze to her face. A pair of sunglasses covered her eyes, but he was still able to make out her high cheekbones and luscious, plump lips. Ethan bit back a laugh at the red fedora sitting atop her head. There was something about her though that pinged in his memory bank. Like he'd met her before, but he couldn't remember where.

The sunglasses lowered, and a flash of blue ice glared at him. "Are you quite finished with your perusal? Do I pass muster? Or do I need to work on something?"

The tone, he'd heard the snappiness before, and it was nothing like her sultry question only seconds ago.

Damn, I wish I could remember.

In his job, he needed to make a quick study of his surroundings and people. Even the most innocent-looking person or object could have a bomb hidden on them. Usually, when he made his observations, he was infinitely more subtle than he had been while checking out Isabella.

"Sorry. Yes. I'm Ethan Masters, and no, you don't need

to work on anything."

Not the best first impression to make on his blind date that was for sure, but he could twist it around so that his last impression was the one that stuck in her mind. He could do with a little distraction while he was stateside, and, for once, Linc hadn't lied.

Ethan slammed the brakes on those thoughts. It was a coffee date and he wasn't a player like Linc. It had been a long while since he'd had anything resembling a serious relationship. Not to say that a long-term relationship didn't interest him. He wanted to settle down, have the wife, house, and kids. He just had to find the right woman who wanted the same future. His mom was constantly dropping hints about not getting any younger and wanting to enjoy her grandchildren.

"Really?" She drawled the word out so it became four syllables instead of two. "Good to know."

Fuck. He should've let her comment slide. He needed to do something to salvage this date, because he would never live it down with the guys, and especially Linc, if word got around he'd struck out yet again. Not to mention he really wanted to find out if they had met before. "I like your hat, which means you're Isabella Knowles. Right?" he asked with a grin and touched his own.

A small answering smile lifted the corners of her lips. "Thank you. I like yours too. And, yes, I'm Isabella."

And like that, they were back on an even keel. He wasn't

usually this inept with women…

He canted his head toward the door of the cafe. "Coffee?"

"Sure, that's what we're here for, isn't it?"

He straightened his spine even more as another burst of familiarity washed over him.

Okay, so maybe they weren't quite on an even keel yet.

Ethan held the door open for her. "After you."

Her exotic, spicy scent teased his nostrils as she brushed past him. It suited her sassy responses to him.

"Why don't you see if you can grab a table, and I'll order for us?" Her raised eyebrow made him quickly add, "Or we can order together and then find a table."

Isabella smiled, a little less frosty than her previous ones. "I'll have a large latte with an extra shot, thanks."

She turned and her skirt lifted, giving him a teasing look at her long, golden legs before it settled down. Her hips swayed as she walked to a vacant table in the corner.

Oh no, it couldn't be, could it?

The way Isabella's skirt floated around her legs unlocked the memory. The movement, then and just now, reminded him of leaves swirling on a gust of wind in the dessert, fierce and free.

Was Isabella Knowles the woman from the mall the other week? The day when one of the largest shopping centers in San Antonio had been evacuated due to a bomb scare. The same woman who'd argued with him about leaving the center because of a small child.

No, it couldn't be. With her hat on, as well as her sunglasses, she looked nothing like the woman who'd argued with him. And it was clear she didn't recognize him either. Guess the Hollywood stars knew something when they donned baseball caps and sunglasses to be incognito.

Maybe he was suffering a bit of sunstroke after standing outside waiting for her to arrive. Yeah, that was it. He was superimposing one event on top of another.

Order placed, he weaved through the tables, carrying a plate with two slices of lemon pound cake. He'd taken a chance that Isabella liked lemon; if not, he'd get her whatever she wanted.

He halted two feet away from the table, Isabella wasn't facing him, so she couldn't see his approach.

Shit, it *was* her—the stubborn woman from the mall. Now that she'd taken her sunglasses and hat off, there was no mistake. Isabella's hair fell in soft curls around her shoulders, some loose strands framing her face like it had the day they'd clashed.

Great, now what do I do?

Stay or go?

Man, working his way around this date was like walking through a minefield. Every step, or in his case today, every word, led to disaster. At least when he had to work a dangerous site he had Sam by his side, guiding him safely through the treacherous ground. Her eagle nose was able to scent out explosives in seconds. Somehow, he didn't think his K-9 partner could sniff her way out of this predicament the date had fallen into.

He wasn't one to bail on a date, unless they failed to show up, so he'd stay and maybe once she recognized him they'd laugh about it and have a good time.

"Drinks will be here shortly," he said as he sat and set the plate down in the middle of the table.

"Ooh, lemon pound cake, my favorite."

Score one for Team Masters.

"Awesome, help yourself."

"Don't mind if I do." She broke off a corner and popped it in her mouth. Her eyes widened—was there something wrong with the cake? She began to cough before swallowing the morsel. "You. It's you. The bossy guy from the mall. Is this some kind of joke?"

Damn, he'd been found out.

"And you're the stubborn woman who argued about leaving."

Her eyes narrowed. "Really? So that's how it's going to be? I don't know why I bothered coming here," she said under her breath, loud enough for him to hear.

Yeah, this was turning out to be another blind date from hell. Never again was he going to consider letting himself be set up.

The date was a bust; might as well blow it up altogether.

"Don't you realize how dangerous it is to ignore evacuation alarms and instructions? That by going off on your own—"

"I'm sorry, who died and put you in charge?"

God, this woman was infuriating, Linc would be getting an earful from him the next time he saw him.

No more bets.

"It's my job to keep people safe. Believe me, I've seen the damage that can be done by someone not following instructions."

The hat was causing his head to itch. He reached up and took it off. Immediately all animation drained from Isabella's face. Ethan scanned the restaurant for any sign of danger. His gaze narrowed on the guy standing by the door, hand in pocket, but he relaxed when the patron pulled out a pack of gum. The other people in the café were either looking at their phones, working on laptops, talking, or gazing out the window. Everything looked harmless.

What on earth had caused her dramatic change? Sure, they'd been having a heated discussion but not enough for her to look as if she'd seen a ghost. In fact, before he took his hat off, it looked like she was about to blast him again.

Wood scraped on tile; Isabella was in the motion of standing. The good manners his mother had drummed into him and the military enhanced made him stand as well.

"Isabella, what's wrong?"

"Nothing's wrong. I just—sorry, Ethan."

She brushed past him and he was, once again, assailed by

her exotic scent that reminded him of incense burning in the night. He stood rooted to the spot for a few seconds, watching as she exited the café as though the hounds of hell were on her tail.

What the hell had just happened?

ISABELLA RUSHED THROUGH the glass door, bumping into someone walking in the coffee shop.

"Sorry," she mumbled as she scrunched her red fedora between her fingers before putting it on her head. So what if she looked stupid, at least it provided some protection from the hot, Texas sun.

Military.

It all made sense. The autocratic tone he used at the mall. His comment about seeing what happened when no one followed instructions. Ethan Masters was in the military.

His hair had been slightly longer when he'd confronted her in the mall, but now she'd recognize the buzz cut he sported anywhere. In fact, she'd seen it on her dad his whole life. The style brought back so many painful memories. It had taken her years to be able to look at her dad without remembering the loss in her life that haircut represented.

What a dumb idea it was to agree to a blind date her dad set up for her. There was a reason she spaced out her visits with him. She should've worked out it had disaster written all over it when he handed her the red fedora. Never had she expected Ethan to be wearing the hat as well; she'd figured he'd hold it. If he had, she would've done a quick about-face and walked away from him before he even saw her. Not just because of the hair, but because of their earlier encounter. She didn't need a bossy man in her life.

The worst thing about the whole situation was, she'd been attracted to Ethan the second she'd clapped eyes on his tall form as he waited out front of the café. For a few heartbeats she'd been looking forward to getting to know him better. It had been so long since she'd been on a date, and the fact her dad had set her up with a guy who was good-looking—well, she thought things in her life were beginning to shift. The last thing on her mind had been checking out what his hair looked like under the hat. In hindsight, it should've been the first thing.

Someone tapped on her shoulder; she screamed at the sudden contact. If Dad could see her, he'd berate her for not being aware of her surroundings.

"Hey, it's me, Ethan. I'm not going to hurt you."

He got that right. No way was she going to give him the opportunity to hurt her physically or emotionally.

"If this is how you act around women, it's no wonder you have to be set up on blind dates."

He flinched, but all she wanted was to get away. Away from the memories that threatened to overwhelm her being around him.

"Our date is the result of one too many tequila shots with a whiskey chaser and a bet I should've ignored. I can assure you I don't need any help getting my own dates." He took a step back, oblivious to the people walking past them, some trying hard not to stare.

She wanted to shout out, "It's okay, go about your business and ignore us."

"Why did you follow me?" she asked.

"You rushed out so quickly, I wanted to make sure you weren't sick or something."

Okay, so maybe she was being over the top, but the second he'd revealed his GI Joeness, she couldn't be near him. "There's no need. As you can see, I'm fine."

"Something spooked you though. I mean, I know we weren't having the most auspicious of discussions, but you didn't have to run out."

Ethan's sincerity wrapped around her. He was a nice, albeit bossy, guy. He just wasn't for her, even if her heart had started beating in a way it hadn't done for a decade.

"I'm sorry, Ethan, you're right, I shouldn't have run out. You seem like a nice guy. But I made a promise to myself that I'd never get involved with someone who was in the military." She stuck out her hand. "Thanks for not standing me up. Good luck with your future."

Oh, my God, could she sound any more formal?

"How do you know I'm in the military?"

His question surprised her. "Um, well, you know, because of your haircut."

He ran his hand through his short, spiky hair. Tall, dark, and handsome. The description was cliché, but it fit Ethan Masters to a *T*. His gray T-shirt hugged his muscles. The faded blue jeans he wore clung to his hips.

"Who's to say I don't like getting my hair cut this way? Maybe I happen to like really short hair."

Had she jumped to conclusions? Sweat beaded her forehead behind the band of the silly hat she still wore, and she gripped her handbag a little tighter.

"Are you telling me that you're not in the armed forces? That I've made a mistake?"

Ethan closed his eyes and his chest rose and fell as he took a deep breath. Her hopes whooshed out of her at the same time. "No, you're right. I'm in the air force."

Disappointment slammed into her gut with the accuracy of a heat-seeking missile. Memories she'd buried roared to the surface. Memories of another time and another military person who had brought her happiness. Memories of when that happiness was ripped away from her and she was left adrift, lost in her pain. She couldn't do that again, no matter how alive she'd felt for a few moments.

"I'm sorry, I can't. Goodbye, Ethan."

Without waiting for a response, she turned her back on him and continued down the sidewalk.

Don't look back.
Don't look back.

Isabella looked back. Ethan stood where she'd left him, his gorgeous mouth twisted in a look of confusion.

Damn, fate was wearing her bitchy pants today.

Chapter Three

THE EARLY MORNING sun glinted through the light cloud cover, casting shadows on the road as Ethan and his unit did their mandatory PT workout. Thank God, Ryder and the other guys hadn't cornered him yet to hear the juicy details about his weekend date. It could be because their lieutenant colonel seemed in a surly mood. Today wasn't the day to push chatting while working out, like they normally did.

It had been three days since he'd met Isabella, and even though their date had been over quicker than Sam scarfing down her breakfast, he still couldn't get the image of her disappointment out of his mind. Her blue eyes, which had sparkled while they'd been sparring, had dulled to a stormy-ocean shade when she'd given him a last look before continuing on her way.

He knew all about the difficulties of being married to a career military person. Hell, his whole family was military. His mom had been in the army; his dad as well. His maternal granddad had been a World War II pilot. It was preordained that Ethan would enlist after high school. It was just a matter of which branch he would join. Instead of being a pilot, he'd chosen to work in security forces and then switched over to the K-9 unit. He loved every minute of it.

His family had supported and encouraged him every step of the way. That was what he wanted from the woman he would end up with. Someone who loved him unconditionally, even when deployed, the way his father loved his mother. He'd yet to find that woman, but Isabella had fired neurons he hadn't known existed in him.

Finally, after a grueling PT session, showered and in his uniform, he headed to the mess hall for some breakfast. Piling up his plate to replace the carbs he lost, he headed to the table where the rest of his squadron sat.

He took one mouthful before the questions started.

"I saw you all zoned out there this morning, Masters. Wet dreaming about blind date Betty?" Ryder teased. "She was that good, huh?"

If the guys could read his mind, they'd have a field day razzing the shit out of him.

"It was fine. We met, had a coffee, and that's it. I won't be seeing her again."

"Who had Ethan strikes out again?" Ryder called out. Seven arms rose in the air.

Ethan picked up his biscuit and tossed it at his buddy, hitting him square on the nose. "You're all assholes." He shook his head and resumed eating to stop himself from laughing.

"Was she hot, or was she a disaster like the last chick Linc set you up with? Ha, maybe Linc is deliberately sabotaging you. What did you do to him?"

Ryder just wouldn't leave it alone. There was no way Ethan was going to share with his buddies that Isabella was indeed hot as Linc had promised. But he had to say something to get them off his back. Maybe saying it out loud would exorcise her face from his memory bank.

Yeah, and that's a pig you see flying past the window.

"Put it this way. Linc didn't lie. Isabella Knowles is good-looking."

Understatement of the century. If he breathed a word that she was stunning, sexy, and spunky, his buddies would all be hassling Linc for a hookup. The least Ethan could do was save them from being shot down by her.

"Isabella doesn't date military guys. So, close your jaws, boys. You have no chance with her."

"Sucks to be you, eh, Ethan?"

"Yeah, Ryder. Sucks to be me. But"—he pointed his fork at Ryder—"at least I got to spend time with a pretty lady, which is more than you've done in months."

Laughter rang out around the table, and conversation turned to other subjects. For the sake of his team, Ethan put the disaster date behind him. Lapses in concentration could get them killed. Even though he was back stateside and on base, his focus needed to be on his job. And not on a woman with captivating blue eyes and luscious blonde hair.

A woman who wanted nothing to do with him.

ISABELLA SHOULD BE marking the paper on her desk, not staring at it. Grading papers was an integral part of the job, and she always stayed after school to get the job done. Once she was home, she liked to relax without the specter of her own homework hanging over her head. It didn't always work out that way, and today looked like it was going to be that day.

Every time she looked at the essay, all she saw was Ethan's face. The slump of his shoulders as she walked away from him. His disappointment was an emotion she didn't understand. Why was he upset their date didn't work out? They'd spent all of twenty minutes together.

Heck, if she considered their first meeting at the mall, all they'd done was clash, yet here she sat, days later, still thinking about the guy.

How pathetic was she? He was the opposite of everything she wanted in a guy.

Her phone buzzed by her elbow, glancing down she saw *Dad* flashing up on the screen. Biting back a groan, Isabella hesitated before picking it up. She'd been expecting this call. Expecting Dad to check in and find out how the date went. It still rankled that he'd knowingly set her up with a guy who was in the military. He was well aware of her reasons for staying far away from anyone involved with any of the armed forces.

Picking up her phone, she swiped the call. "Hey, Dad."

"Hi, Isabella, how's your day?"

Casual conversation from her dad? This wasn't normal. Perhaps he figured out he'd mucked up by setting her up on a date. Over the years, their relationship had gone through many cycles, starting with resentment that his career in the army ripped her away from the friends she made and caused her mother to walk out on them. Then gratitude that he was there when she needed him most.

At present they were going through a strained period, and, with the way she was currently feeling toward her father, it was going to stay that way for a while.

"I'm glad it's over. What can I do for you, Dad?" She deliberately kept her voice cool.

A sigh sounded down the phone. Perhaps she didn't need to be so hard on him, but Dad knew everything she'd gone through with Travis.

"I wanted to know how your date went."

"I think you know exactly how it went, Dad."

"You didn't give him a chance, did you?"

"Why on earth would I? You know how I feel about going out with someone in the military." Her voice rose a couple of octaves with every word. If she didn't lower her voice, the remaining staff at the school would hear her business. Apart from her best friend, Meredith, who worked at the school with her, she didn't want her colleagues to know everything about her past. Some things were better left unsaid. And her short marriage was one of them.

"So I take it there won't be another date with this man?"

Honestly, what was wrong with Dad? Couldn't he hear how upset she was? "No, there will not. If he had been in any occupation other than the military, I might have given him a chance."

"Isabella, you've hardly been living since Travis's accident."

"I can't believe you went there, Dad. Travis was my life and he was taken from me in a flash. I'm not going to put myself through that again."

"You need to put yourself out there, Daughter, not hide away."

Isabella wanted to pull her hair out. Yeah, it was going to be a while before she talked to her dad again. "Look, I've got to go, Dad. I'll talk to you later." Much later, but she left that unsaid.

"Before you hang up, I've got one last thing to say."

"Yes?"

"I didn't raise you to be a coward. I dare you to ask him out again."

"What? Since when did you dare me to do anything?"

"Since now. I don't like to see you shut yourself away."

"Oh, my God, I'm not shutting myself away, and I'm not going to do this with you. Bye, Dad." She disconnected the call and tossed her phone on her table, holding her breath as it slid across the wood surface, stopping just before toppling off.

What had got into him?

Sure, he'd always pushed her to excel at school, and yes, when her world fell apart he provided her with all the support she needed. Once she was ready, she'd gone to college and gotten her degree, and now she was living her life the way she wanted. She didn't need her dad setting her up with anyone.

Her phone chimed with an incoming text message; sighing, she leaned over and grabbed her phone. The second she saw the message she wished she hadn't.

"Here's Ethan's number: 825 555 9830."

Seriously? Her dad wasn't giving up on this. Why was he so invested in her contacting Ethan? He hadn't even met the guy.

"Hey, are you just about done?"

Isabella looked up and saw Meredith, standing in the doorway. "Not even close," she said. Looked like it was going to be a long night for her.

"What's wrong?" Meredith plonked herself down in one of the student chairs.

"My dad."

"Ahh, what's he done this time?"

Meredith had been her friend since college days. Both of

them had started later than normal due to circumstances beyond their control. They'd been assigned as roommates and had connected the second they took their first class together. It helped they'd both had traumatic events in their pasts, so when one of them was down, the other knew how to bring them out of their funk.

"I told you about the date he set me up on?"

"Yeah, and how the guy turned out to be the same one from the mall. So I'm sure, once you explained all of that, he understood why you don't want to see him again."

Isabella shifted in her seat. She'd been so annoyed with her dad she hadn't mentioned their first meeting. "Not quite. I just asked him why he would think it was a good idea to set me up with someone in the military after he knew what I went through."

"Ouch. I bet that went down well."

"That's an understatement. He basically dared me to call Ethan and set up another date. What does he think, I'm thirteen and desperate? What sort of parent does that to their kid, especially when said child is almost thirty years old?"

Meredith smiled, but it didn't reach her eyes. "Just be grateful you have a parent who cares."

Isabella's annoyance died in a heartbeat. Meredith had lost both her parents in car accident when she was young. She had to fight for her own life, and her best friend had done an amazing job. "You're right. I'm sorry, Mere. I should be grateful that Dad cares."

"It's fine. I know you didn't mean it. So what are you going to do? Are you going to call Ethan?"

Isabella should've known Meredith would brush off her comment as nothing. It was what she did and what Isabella did when thinking about her past, which was something she tried hard not to do on a regular basis. "I have his number; Dad just texted it to me. As for whether I'll call him, I don't know."

"Maybe your dad is right. Maybe you should give this guy another chance."

Isabella's eyes almost bugged out of her head. "What? You know what happened to Travis. Why do you think I should put myself through that kind of hurt and worry again?"

Meredith shrugged. "You told me it was a freak accident. A one-in-a-million chance of it happening again. Just think about it, Iz. Have some fun for a change."

"Maybe."

Meredith's phone rang and a smile lit her face. "Oh, it's Mark. I've got to take this. I'm here if you want to talk."

Her friend dashed out the door, saying a breathless hello to her boyfriend, who was on the other side of the world, no doubt closing in on another business deal.

Picking up her phone, Isabella sat back and studied the number in her dad's message. Why was she even considering dialing it? They'd hardly said anything to each other, and what they did say was heated and far from an amenable conversation.

Yet during the short time in the coffee shop, she'd been energized in a way she hadn't been for a long time. Without a doubt, if Ethan weren't in the military, she'd be calling him.

So why don't you? You've got nothing to lose. Take a chance, Isabella. One date. That's all it has to be. One date.

Who knew the voice in her head could be so reasonable, but it was. Plus, she had an idea her dad expected her not to take him up on his dare. So why not show him he read her all wrong? Show him she could go on a date with a military man and then walk away without looking back.

Before she could talk herself out of it, Isabella pressed the blue, underlined numbers and confirmed she did indeed want to call the number listed.

The phone rang two times. "Ethan Masters."

All thought drifted out of her mind at the husky, masculine voice. Did it sound that delicious when she sat opposite him?

"Hello? Is this you, Linc? If you're trying to do a heavy-breathing call, you suck."

"It's not Linc." Her voice broke on the last word and she mentally slapped herself upside her head. She wasn't a pathetic, scared girl—no matter what her father might think. She cleared her throat. "It's Isabella Knowles."

Silence stretched down the line, and for a few seconds, she wondered if the call had dropped.

"Isabella Knowles, of the shopping mall and red fedora blind date Isabella?" There was a trace of humor in his voice, mixed with a tinge of surprise.

"One and the same."

"Well, this is unexpected. I kind of got the impression you didn't think too much of me."

Isabella pinched the bridge of her nose and closed her eyes. Had she really thought it was going to be easy to call up a guy she'd met twice? It was time to man up, as her father would often say. "I'd like to apologize for the way I acted. I shouldn't have run out on you like that."

He chuckled, and the sound slithered down her spine. "No, you shouldn't have, but I'm sure there is a perfectly good explanation."

"There is." An explanation he wasn't going to get. For the last decade, she'd successfully avoided talking about Travis and her short marriage with strangers.

So she left it hanging.

"But I don't warrant knowing it."

"Correct." Geez, this was as disastrous as their other two encounters. Surely, this was fate telling her that asking Ethan out on another date was a bad idea.

I dare you to.

Her father's words drifted into her mind. Okay, maybe it would be different face-to-face this time. "Do you want to meet up for a drink?" She blurted the words out in a flurry and hoped like hell it made sense.

"Are you asking me out on another date, Ms. Knowles?"

Thank God she was on the phone. At least that way Ethan didn't have to see her embarrassment. Her cheeks burned and she guessed they were tomato red, a color that never looked good on her.

"What if I am?" she sassed back.

"Then I'd say yes, but…"

For a split second, elation welled inside of her, an emotion she didn't understand given her reluctance to see him again. "But?"

"I have your number now; I'll be in touch with time and place. How about that?"

"Seriously, you're going all macho on me because I asked you out. You have to pick the place?" Okay, so maybe her first impression of him had been correct—he was a controlling ass.

"No, I just need to check my schedule. I'm sure my weekend is free, but I want to confirm before I make plans."

Okay, talk about making assumptions. Seemed she was doing a pretty good job of always thinking badly about Ethan. "Sorry. I jump to conclusions around you. Not something I normally do."

Ethan laughed again. "Guess I'm lucky then. I'll be in touch, okay?"

"Sure, sounds good."

"Bye, Izzy. Your call brightened my day."

"Bye," she murmured.

The enormity of what she'd done hit her the second she laid her phone on the table. She'd agreed to see a military guy again when she'd sworn off them.

What was she thinking?

Relax. The little voice in her head piped up. *You've got this.*

Yes, she did. This was just a date. A simple let's-have-a-drink date. Not an *I-want-to-marry-you* date. If it turned out to be another disaster, she could walk away, never to see him again.

It wasn't a lifelong commitment.

She could remember that, couldn't she?

Chapter Four

ETHAN CHECKED HIS watch for the fifth time. Had he done the right thing by not insisting on picking Isabella up? After the way their conversations had gone in the past, he hadn't wanted to press the issue. With their track record, it was probably safer if she made her own way to the Casa Del Sanchez. That way, both had their own mode of transport, if needed.

Which he hoped they wouldn't need. Third time being the charm and all. He was determined to get to know her better. He'd tried to put her out of his mind, but she'd been front and center since her call more than a week ago.

Unfortunately, Linc had overheard him making arrangements with Isabella and had been unbearable, gloating that he was a matchmaker extraordinaire. Ethan wasn't sure that was a moniker he'd be happy with, but Linc could have it.

Of course, he had to go blab to everyone, so the rest of his team got in on giving Ethan hell about his upcoming date, too. It wouldn't surprise him if there was yet another bet going around to see if he struck out again. God, he hoped he didn't. Isabella made him think things he hadn't thought of in a long time. Why her, he had no idea, but she sparked memories of dreams he'd long ago pushed aside for his desire to succeed in his career.

It was now a half an hour after the time they were supposed to meet. Great, not only had he crashed and burned on the first date, he was now being stood up on their second. With his track record, he should probably give up on dating. Maybe he could talk to the powers that be and ask if he could adopt Sam when she reached retirement age. At least then he'd be assured of a constant companion. One who wouldn't stand him up on a date.

The Riverwalk was full of people heading out for Friday night drinks and dinner. It was impossible to make out if anyone resembled Isabella among the throng.

Time to cut his losses and head back home. He was lucky his roommate was quiet and didn't want to talk much. Caleb was going through a tough time, so Ethan respected his need for space.

"Oh, my God, Ethan, I'm so sorry I'm late."

He whirled around. Strands of hair had escaped Isabella's high ponytail and kissed her cheeks and neck. There was a hint of pink to her face. She looked more stunning than she had the first day he saw her. Her chest was rising and falling against the fabric of the sundress she was wearing, as if she'd run to meet him.

"I was beginning to think I'd been stood up. Are you

okay?"

Dude, why did I go and say that? No one wanted to be reminded that they were late. "Sorry, that first part was rude. But I meant the second part. Is everything okay?"

Yep, now that was a good comeback. Apologize and show concern. All good attributes his mama had taught him.

"No, it's fine. You don't have to apologize. I should've called you or sent a text that I was caught up. There was an accident on the highway and traffic was at a standstill."

"I'm glad you're okay and all that matters is you're here now. Shall we go?" He crooked his elbow and smiled when she placed her arm through his.

"Yep, let's do this."

So far, so good. She hadn't walked away after his opening barb. Perhaps there was hope for them after all. Well, at least for having a good date tonight.

The mass of people surrounding them had thinned, but from experience, he knew, in a few minutes the area would be packed again. Hopefully, they wouldn't have to wait for a table. He navigated them around a group of people to get to the front desk.

"Hi, can I help you?" the hostess asked.

"I was hoping to get a table for two." He could use his military status to try to jump up the queue and get a table immediately, but it never made him comfortable to use his job that way. He served his country with pride and honor. Being able to see all these people walk freely around the

Riverwalk, laughing and happy without having to worry if they would get shot around the corner, was all the thanks he needed.

The girl tapped her tablet before looking up at him. "I'm sorry, we don't have anything available for about fifteen minutes."

Ethan looked at Isabella. "You okay to wait that long? We can always go somewhere else if you want."

"Oh no, that's fine. Besides, if I hadn't been late, we wouldn't have had to wait."

The hostess had an indulgent smile on her face.

"Well, I guess you heard. We're happy to wait."

She laughed. "Yes, I did." The woman handed him a disk with two red lights flashing intermittently. "It will buzz when your table is ready. In the meantime, you can always go and grab a drink at the bar."

Ethan nodded his thanks. "Shall we head to the bar?" he asked Isabella.

Her eyebrow rose and the corner of her lips lifted in a small smile. "Sure, that's what we're here for, isn't it? A drink?"

"Well, yes, that's true. This place also serves delicious food. I thought we might get something to eat as well," he said as he led her to the bar.

"Well, that's a little presumptuous and risky, isn't it?" She winked.

Sure, it was sneaky, but he wanted to make the most of

this night. He wanted to show her that while, yes, the military was his job, there was more to him than his career.

"I'm all about taking risks," he responded. The sparkle in her eyes dimmed, and he could've kicked himself. Isabella extracted her arm from his hold and took a step back.

Good one, Masters. You want to convince her to see you again, not run in the other direction.

"Well, let's just have a drink and see what happens, shall we?"

A blast of artic air circulated around them now, most of it coming from Isabella's words. Great, he was really bombing out here, again. The chances of her staying to eat once their table was ready were looking pretty slim.

A third date? Well, he'd have to work very hard for that one to happen.

The bar was busy, so it took a couple of minutes before the bartender was able to serve them.

"What can I get you?" he asked.

"I'll have a classic mojito, thanks," Isabella said.

"I'll have a Stella," Ethan responded.

Ethan wracked his brain while they waited on their drinks, trying to come up with something witty to bring some life back to their conversation. He kept coming up blank.

Fortunately, the barman pushed their drinks toward them. Out of the corner of his eye, he saw Isabella reach for her purse. No way. It was old-fashioned and he was all for independent women—hell, some of the strongest people he'd seen when he'd been deployed were women—but this was a date, and though he might not have technically asked her out, he was still paying.

However, he could word it in a way as to suggest he wasn't going to be a total caveman. "I'll get this round." He reached into his back pocket and pulled out his wallet, placing a twenty on the bar. As he received his change, the buzzer went off, signaling their table was ready. Maybe once they sat down he could get his mojo back and this date wouldn't turn into a disaster.

Man, if the guys at the base found out he'd bombed a second time he'd never live it down. He'd ask for a two-year deployment; maybe by the time he returned, his abysmal dating life would be forgotten.

Once they were seated and the hostess walked away, Ethan took a long draft of his beer.

"I contemplated wearing my red fedora," he blurted out. Where the hell did that come from? He hadn't even considered wearing that damn hat again. But Isabella laughed and his shoulders relaxed.

"That would've been quite the statement. I suppose it was less clichéd than carrying a red rose. People would wonder if you were filming an episode of *The Bachelor*."

"Oh, please, don't tell me that you actually watch that show."

A delicate shade of pink bloomed on her cheeks. Well

now, how interesting. Isabella watched reality television shows. Was she a closet romantic as well? "I could lie and say I've seen the ads, but, yes, I watch the show. It's quite comical really, all those girls claiming to fall in love in two days while living in the same house with twelve other women. Not to mention television cameras following them everywhere. Very unrealistic."

Okay, so maybe not a romantic after all. But if she wasn't, why watch the show at all? Hmm, there was a little mystery to Isabella. He wouldn't mind unravelling it all. "And yet it does happen."

"What? People falling in love in two days? Or love on a television show being real?" She canted her head and lifted her drink. His body stirred to life when her lips closed around the straw.

"Well, I agree on a television show it's unlikely, but yes, I do believe it can happen in real life. It happened with my parents. My dad said the first time he looked at my mom, she was it for him and vice versa."

If he were being totally truthful with himself, he was beginning to think his parents were an anomaly. Then again, the woman sitting opposite him had fried his senses quicker than an egg on a hot plate. Something that hadn't happened to him before.

"Well, that's great for them. Life isn't a fairy tale, and not all marriages last a lifetime. Some end before they've even had a chance to begin."

When he said he wanted to start a conversation, this wasn't the type he figured they'd have. An edge had crept into her voice. Had she been married? Did her husband cheat on her? Many questions floated through his brain, questions he had no place asking. No matter how much he wanted to.

"You're right. Life isn't a fairy tale. Trust me, I've seen plenty to corroborate this. But life's not worth living if you don't have hope of some sort."

"I agree. The kids I teach give me hope. The way they look at the world is so fresh. You kind of forget that you were once that innocent."

Now this was a perfect lead-in to steer the conversation away from the topic of marriage, divorce, and the ugly aspects of life. "Tell me the moment you knew teaching was the right path for you."

Her job seemed a far safer topic of conversation than her personal life. Things were going well, and he didn't want to jeopardize their date. The more he talked with Isabella, the more he was beginning to like her.

ISABELLA PICKED UP her glass again and gulped another large swallow through her straw. It wasn't a difficult question to answer, just one she didn't really know the answer to. So she went directly for the truth. "I kind of fell into teaching, you could say."

Before Ethan could respond, a waitress turned up at their table, and Isabella said a silent prayer he would forget what they'd been talking about. She was never comfortable talking about herself, especially her road to college. When she'd finished high school, her whole life had been planned out. She was going to be a military wife and mother. Follow her man from base to base. How quickly that had all changed. Now, here she was surrounded by children—only none were hers.

"Do you want to get some guacamole or chips and salsa? Or would you prefer something else?" Ethan asked.

"Umm, I'm happy with whatever you'd like to order." She sat back the second the words left her mouth. On her very rare previous dates, she'd never let the guy order for her. Not to mention she hadn't committed to having something to eat with him, and yet here she was, letting him take the lead.

Huh.

She remained silent while Ethan placed their appetizer order and the waitress left them alone again. Although how alone could they really be in a restaurant full of people?

"What were we talking about before we were interrupted?" Ethan asked.

Could she slip a change of conversation into the mix? Sheesh, what was wrong with her? Being around Ethan had her totally off-kilter. He had an intensity about him she'd never experienced from another person before, not even Travis. Like his interest wasn't just for the sake of making inane conversation.

That was an eye-opener, for sure. This was their first—well, okay, second—date and already it had a different vibe to it than all her previous dates combined. Should she end this one now, before he started expecting more? Or was she the one expecting more?

It's not like you're going to marry the guy.

Her very vocal conscience was correct, and what did it matter if she told Ethan more about how she got into teaching than she'd ever told anyone before?

"Hey, Izzy, are you okay?"

Oh, geez, she'd flaked out again on him. "Yeah, I'm fine, just having a mental conversation with myself."

Oh, my God, why did I say that out loud?

"Well, that says a lot for my conversations skills if you have to have one with yourself."

Fortunately, he was smiling and, boy, did his smile hit her right in the gut. She really should relax and stop overthinking everything. Acting on instinct, she reached out and placed her hand over his. A sizzle of electricity zigzagged its way through her blood. "I'm sorry. I've been a little vague since I've sat down with you. I'm nervous, I guess."

Ding. Ding. Ding. All the bells went off in her mind like a slot machine hitting the jackpot in a Vegas casino. She *was* nervous, and she didn't know why.

"Will it make you feel better if I say I'm nervous too?" Ethan turned his hand and laced his fingers with hers. The touch was nice and natural. She could get used to this very quickly if she weren't careful.

"Yes, it does." With her free hand she took another sip of her drink. "You asked me how I got into teaching?"

"I did."

How did she explain the fog she was in when she walked onto the college campus? That part she would skip over.

"Well, like I said, I kind of fell into it, to be totally honest. I went to college with no clear vision of what I wanted to do. After the first semester, I went to the academic adviser to see if I could get some, you know, advice."

He chuckled.

"Anyway, she pointed out that I'd picked subjects that would help me get a teaching degree. My grades were good, too, so it was clear that I enjoyed what I was studying."

"Sounds like your subconscious mind knew exactly what you wanted to do but hadn't let you in on the secret yet."

Isabella laughed. "Certainly seemed that way." She took a deep breath and asked the question she wasn't quite sure she truly wanted the answer to. "How about you—did you always want to be in the military? Or was it like me, something you fell into?"

Ethan sat back, breaking their physical touch, as the waitress arrived with their appetizers. "No, I didn't fall into it. My whole family is military. My mom was in the army but doesn't talk about it much. When I was eight, Dad told me the story of how she'd stayed with a family until they were rescued after being trapped in a partially collapsed building. How she put her own life on the line with bullets ricocheting off the building around her, but she wasn't going to leave that family. Hearing the story confirmed what I already knew—I'd follow the family tradition and enlist after graduation. I chose air force instead of army."

The corn chip she'd just taken a bite of lodged in her throat, and she picked up her drink, sucking as much liquid as she could. Of course, she'd go on a date with a guy whose whole family lived and breathed everything military—after all, her father set her up on the blind date initially. He only knew people who lived and breathed army life. Or, in Ethan's case, air force. "By your whole family, do you mean everyone or just your mom and dad?"

Ethan chuckled, the sound light, and it sent shivers trickling down her spine. "Yeah, everyone, including my granddad and grandma. I think a couple of aunts didn't go into the military, but their kids have."

She should definitely run in the other direction after this dinner date was over. It was bad enough with only her father. No way could she take on a whole family.

Problem was, she was beginning to like Ethan. Despite the awkward start to their date tonight, she was enjoying herself, the conversation they were sharing, the light touches of his hand against hers.

"What happened when you were born? Your mom wouldn't have been able to deploy or anything."

"When the time came around for Mom to reenlist a few years after she and Dad got married, they discussed it and Mom decided not to."

"Did she resent that? I mean, after the story you told me, and if she loved being in the military, wouldn't she have felt annoyed that she had to give up her career to have kids?"

Ethan scooped up a dollop of guac and popped it in his mouth. The action shouldn't have been attractive, but it was. After he swallowed, he picked up their conversation. "No, Mom was ready for a change." He paused and swallowed some beer. "Her reenlistment date came up just after the incident I told you about. After discussing things, they decided they wanted to try for a family. It wasn't hard for her to decide to step away from the army. Although I can't remember how many direct party companies she worked for as I was growing up, she did Mary Kay, Tupperware, and some that are no longer in business."

At least there was one Masters who wasn't entrenched in the military world. Wait, that wasn't true. Her son was active, and in all likelihood, her husband could still be involved as well.

Isabella reached for her drink and found it empty. Geez, she really needed a shot of rum now to dull the thoughts running around her mind like a hamster on a wheel.

Ethan was standing before she could put her glass down again. "What? Is something wrong?" she asked. Had Ethan seen something dangerous? She swiveled to check out the restaurant, but to her eye it looked like everyone was caught up in their own worlds.

"No, everything's fine. I'm just going to get you a drink. It will be quicker if I go to the bar and get it for you instead of waiting for the waitress." He paused and looked down at her. "You look like you need it now rather than later."

Ugh, every time she thought she had some control over the situation, that she could walk away from Ethan, he went and did something like this. Something so sweet and out of the blue.

"Thanks, but instead of a mojito, I'll just have a Coke. I have to drive."

"One Coke coming right up." He looked at her and then the door. "You'll still be here when I get back, right?"

"Um, yeah, unless you don't want me to be."

He rubbed a hand down his face. Well, seeing as how she'd grabbed for her drink when he'd talked about his family, his was a natural reaction.

Reaching out, she touched the hand holding her glass. "Yes, Ethan. I'll still be here. Maybe when you get back we can look at the menu and order some more food."

His smile widened, and she couldn't deny the sight left her a little breathless.

Oh dear, she could be getting herself into trouble. But maybe it would be a good trouble. Perhaps she needed to leave her fears behind and live in the moment.

Chapter Five

E THAN REFRAINED FROM grabbing Isabella's hand as they stepped out of the restaurant. After his embarrassing, teenage *will you still be here?* outburst, the rest of the evening had gone well. So well he hadn't wanted it to end, but when their waitress came past their table for a fifth time and finally gave him the *can you please leave so I can get more tips?* look, he'd taken the hint.

The air was still warm, but not oppressively so, and there was a slight breeze. The sidewalks were full of people enjoying their Friday night get-togethers.

"Do you want to take a cruise around the Riverwalk?" he asked.

"Sure, sounds fun. It's a nice night for it."

When a group of laughing teenagers jostled her, he stopped fighting his instincts and took hold of her hand. Her step faltered for a moment, but then she continued on. In fact, she moved a little closer to him.

By the time they reached the area to board the boat, Isabella had relaxed and had wrapped her other arm around his, her exotic perfume surrounding him. He had to mentally go through the commands he gave Sam during a training session to stop his body from reacting to her touch.

"Have you ever done this cruise before?" he asked as other people climbed onboard and settled around them.

"Nope, this is my first time."

"Really? How long have you lived in San Antonio?"

"A couple of years. I mean, I've thought about doing it but just never got around to it. It always seemed so crowded when I walked past the ticketing areas."

"Please tell me you've at least gone to the Alamo."

The sound of her laugh traveled down his spine and through his bloodstream. "Of course, I have. I'm a teacher. The Alamo is always on the excursion list. Particularly for fifth graders."

The boat pulled away from the dock and puttered down the river. The guide was giving his general welcome talk. Ethan had heard it a couple of times, so he didn't need to listen to it again. Besides, he wanted to keep talking to Isabella. He leaned close so the folks around him wouldn't hear. "What was your first impression?"

"Shh, I'm trying to listen." She turned her head and, because he was so close, their noses brushed together gently. This close, he could make out the blues in her eyes. The long length of her eyelashes. Her lips were so close to his, all it would take was for him to move half an inch. He'd be able to fulfill his wish since he'd first seen her—to see how she tasted.

"Izzy," he whispered. Her eyes widened a fraction, and her breath hitched audibly. Instead of kissing her, he tapped her nose lightly. "Sorry. I'll let you listen."

Ethan straightened and put a little distance between them, although their legs still touched from thigh to knee. Once the guide finished his introduction, Ethan returned to the conversation they were having. "So, back to the Alamo. What did you think when you first saw it?"

A soft smile played across her lips and a faraway look entered her eyes. "I've read the history books and seen the movie, but to actually walk inside... it filled me with a sense of reality. People died in those small rooms while others huddled for their lives. It wasn't just a movie. It wasn't something that you read about in a book. A group of men and women sacrificed their lives in the name of freedom. The bullet holes on the outside of the building are a testament to that fact."

"It's hard to imagine the barren lands that surrounded the building when you look at how the city of San Antonio has sprung up around it. Visiting it never gets old."

"You're so right. As I said, I've been there a few times now on school excursions. The younger kids just see a building, but they really don't take in the enormity of what happened there. Plus, they're too young to show them the Alamo movie. Don't think their parents would appreciate it too much."

Ethan laughed. "Yeah, probably wouldn't go down well."

Their voices trailed off as the guide pointed out other points of interest, like Casa Rio, the first restaurant to open up on the Riverwalk. How the Riverwalk was conceived as a way to minimize future flood damage after a major flood in the 1920s. After an hour, they returned to the dock, and both waited until the other passengers had disembarked before they moved from their seats.

Ethan wanted to prolong having Isabella by his side, holding her close. For him, the date had been successful and an experience he'd like to do again. He hoped Isabella felt the same way. But assuming could lead him into a wealth of problems. He didn't know if she even wanted another date with him. He'd be disappointed if she didn't, but if that was the case then so be it.

Once they were back on the Riverwalk, he opened his mouth a couple of times, but he didn't quite know what to say.

"Do you want to walk to the Alamo? I'm parked near there," Isabella said.

Was there a hint of hope in her voice? Could he assume, just a little, she'd enjoyed herself, too, and didn't want the night to end? "Sure, I was going to ask where you were parked."

Ethan put his arm around her shoulder and held her close as they walked through the crowd toward the Alamo. Neither spoke. Once they reached the building, they stopped and looked at the lit-up limestone structure. Even at night, a crowd of people studied the plaques dotted around the perimeter of the path leading to the building.

"Do you ever wonder what was going through their minds during the battle?" Isabella asked.

Her question was innocent, but it struck close to home. Every time he was deployed, he couldn't stop the *what ifs*. What if this time he didn't make it back? What if he got injured? What if something happened to Sam? They were a partnership and it was up to them to ensure the safety of the guys at his back.

"I—" His voice broke on the single syllable. He cleared his throat and tried again. "Their hearts would've been beating out of their chests, and their palms would've been wet with sweat. Some would've been thinking about how to protect the women and children huddling in the back rooms, while others would be keeping watch and see the soldiers advancing. As the gunfire got louder and the man next to them was shot to death, the hopelessness of the situation would've sunk in. Their fear and the instinct to run and save themselves would've been a hard fight to win, but they beat it down. They knew what they had to do. They were fighting for their freedom. Everyone who fought in the *Battle of the Alamo* was well aware the odds of surviving were slim. Eventually, a sense of inevitability would've settled over them. They were outnumbered, and death was one shot away. Just like today's military personnel."

"I don't know how they did it," Isabella whispered.

"How *you* do it?"

He pulled her close, wrapping his arms around her, reveling in the fact she wound her arms around him. "I serve my country and I know the risks. My job keeps the kids you're teaching safe and able to sleep at night without fear."

"You probably get sick of people asking you about why you went into the military."

Ethan reached between them and lifted her chin so he could look into her eyes. "You can ask me anything. Anything about my job and I will answer the questions."

The silence stretched between them. Had he pushed too far? He still didn't understand her reticence to dating someone who was in the military. Hell, he didn't even know if they would have a third date.

A group of teenagers walked past, laughing and joking, breaking the spell that had befallen them.

"I should probably go home," she murmured. "It's getting late."

Ethan nodded. "Where's your car?"

"In the multistory lot around the corner."

"Let me walk you to your car."

Isabella nodded, and he once again popped his arm around her shoulder, smiling when her hand slipped into the back pocket of his jeans.

Standing beside her car five minutes later, beads of sweat dotted his brow and palms—and not from the short walk to her vehicle. His blood pounded in his ears. He wanted badly to kiss her.

Isabella extracted her hand from his jeans pocket and dug in her purse for her keys. He missed the warmth of her touch.

"Well," she started and looked up at him.

There was a gleam in her eye as she angled herself a little closer to him. Almost a wish. Without second-guessing what he was about to do, he leaned down and placed his lips over hers.

She shuffled a little closer; her arms wound around his neck and he hooked his other one loosely around her waist. Their lips danced to a sweet, silent tune. Her mouth opened to deepen the kiss and he took advantage, slipping his tongue inside. A soft moan whispered out of her.

Ethan made himself pull away slowly. He touched his lips to hers for a brief moment before stepping back. "I had a really nice time tonight, Izzy."

"Me too. Umm…" She looked up at the roof and then back at him.

What he wanted to do was ask her out again. For the first time in, hell, he couldn't even remember when, he wanted to do more than just have a couple of casual dates that ended up nowhere. He wanted to spend as much free time as he could getting to know the beautiful teacher in front of him while he waited for his next deployment orders. The big question was—did she want the same or was she about to brush him off?

"Do you want to come over for dinner one night?" The words rushed out of her mouth in a torrent.

He inwardly fist-pumped. "I'd really like that." He managed to keep his voice casual so as not to give away how excited he was by the prospect of spending more time with her.

"Great. How about tomorrow?" Her eyes widened.

"You already regret saying that, don't you?" he responded, chuckling. He should be offended by her reaction, but he wasn't. He was only glad she had agreed to another date.

Fortunately, she laughed and shrugged. "Maybe, but how about it? Dinner at my place? I promise not to poison you."

"Sounds like a plan."

Her mouth might have said the words, but her eyes still held a startled deer-in-headlights look.

If he was into betting, he'd lay odds tomorrow he'd get a text canceling dinner.

Chapter Six

"WHAT WAS I thinking?" Isabella muttered as she picked up the pieces of the bowl that had shattered on the floor. The only time she wore a maxi dress and it got covered in crushed avocado.

Last night, she'd clearly been caught up in the fog of Ethan's kiss. Why else would she have asked him over to dinner? They'd ended up having such a nice night together, which surprised the heck out of her. Now confusion rode through her senses and she'd questioned her sanity many times during the day.

It had been a miracle she'd been able to drive herself home with the thoughts of Ethan and his kiss that had taken up residence in her head. Her mind had been blown away totally by the sensual touch of his lips on hers. Her body had craved more, a longing she hadn't experienced in a very long time.

Of course, her dreams starred Ethan and his lips. The dreams had started off sweet and sexy and then they'd turned sinister with a dark shadow looming over Ethan. She'd awakened with her heart racing and her body covered in sweat. Falling back to sleep had been a chore, and when she finally managed it, well, her dreams didn't bear remembering.

What she should've done was follow through on her thoughts and text Ethan to cancel their dinner date the second she got up. Every time she picked up her phone, opened her message app, her finger had hovered over his name for a couple of seconds before she put the phone down. Texting to cancel anything was a cheat's way out of doing things. The problem was, if she called him, the sound of his voice in her ear would send her plans of cancellation flying out the window.

Now here she was, a half an hour before Ethan was due to arrive, cleaning up homemade guacamole off the floor. She still had to change, too. At least the lasagna she'd made was in the oven. There would be nothing worse if that were the dish she'd dropped. They'd been eating takeout.

With one last swipe of a cloth, the mess was cleaned up. So, they'd have salsa and chips to snack on before dinner instead.

Isabella raced to her room, whipping the dress over her head and tossing it into the hamper as she passed it on her way to her closet. It had taken her ages to decide what to wear, and now she had to come up with another outfit in five minutes.

She reached in and grabbed the first thing she spied, another sundress, similar to the one she'd had on the previous evening. There was no time to debate whether it was perfect or not. Ethan would be arriving any minute now and the last thing she wanted to be doing was zipping herself up while answering the door.

The doorbell rang as she was coming out of the bathroom after touching up her makeup. The butterflies in her stomach turned into a herd of stampeding elephants.

She took a deep breath before reaching for the doorknob and twisting it open. Her heart skipped a beat when she clapped eyes on Ethan. Like the previous evening, he was dressed in jeans and a button-down shirt, the light tan color accentuating his brown eyes.

"Hi," he said after a few heartbeats. A flush of heat suffused her cheeks; she'd been staring at him.

"Hey, come in." Isabella took a step back to allow him to enter her house. Their eyes clashed and her fingers gripped the door a little tighter.

His musky scent enveloped her and she swayed toward him. She couldn't deny her growing attraction for the man standing in front of her. It seemed the feeling was mutual. Ethan leaned down and closed the small gap between them. His warm lips landed on hers in another one of his sweet kisses.

Only their lips were touching, but it was enough to ignite a fire inside of her. How the heck was she going to survive the night without jumping his bones? Never had she wanted to sleep with someone after just meeting them.

BLIND DATE BET

Meredith would tell her to go for it. Then again, her best friend grasped life with both hands after almost dying in a car crash as a teenager.

Ethan broke the kiss and smiled, and her already weak knees went a little weaker. "Well, that's certainly one way to say hello," she said as she closed her door.

"It's the way all hellos should be."

Isabella headed down the hallway to her kitchen. "If that's how you say hello to everyone you meet, we could have some issues."

Ethan laughed. "Yeah, the guys generally run in the opposite direction when they see me arrive at work."

She shook her head, enjoying their banter. "Can't say my fellow colleagues, or parents, would enjoy me saying hello that way. Although some of the single dads might."

Oh, shit, why would she say something like that?

"Hmm, get hit on by a few of the dads, do you?"

She opened the fridge and shoved her face inside, hoping the cool air would reduce the heat enflaming her cheeks. After a few moments, her self-control in hand, she grabbed the salsa and closed the door. "No. I've never been hit on by any parent, single or otherwise, but I know a couple of teachers who have."

"Well, I'm glad for your sake, but those dads must be blind."

He was being sweet, but the whole topic made her uncomfortable. "Let's not talk about this anymore. There's

57

something wrong with the discussion."

Ethan smiled as he dipped a corn chip into her home-made salsa. "You're right. Sorry if I made you uncomfortable." He crunched down on his chip, and she paused, her own chip midair. She liked her salsa with a bit of a bite, so she always added more spices than most people. "Oh, wow, this is good." He grabbed another chip and dug out a big dollop of the tomato mixture.

"Good, and there was supposed to be guacamole, but I dropped the bowl, so salsa it is."

Ethan waved away her comments as he reached for the glass of water she placed in front of him. He drank down most of the glass. "Your salsa packs some punch."

"I know. I like to spice it up more than most people."

His eyebrow rose at her comment, but he let it slide and finished off his water. The timer on the oven went off and she breathed a sigh of relief.

"Do you need any help?" he asked as she opened the oven door, taking a step back to let the steam rise and swirl in the air.

"Nope, I've got it all under control." She placed the steaming lasagna pan on top of her cooktop. "I thought we'd eat outside. The sun sets at the front of the house, so the back patio is cooler now."

"Okkkaaayyy."

She turned to look at him. "Is something wrong?"

"This is going to sound super wimpy considering my job

and all, but I hate bugs."

Isabella stood there for half a second before laughing. "You hate bugs? Kind of hard to avoid when you're in the middle of the desert."

A cute shade of red filtered up Ethan's face. He was the total opposite of what she knew a military man to be. She'd expected him to be arrogant, all *look at me*. She'd seen plenty of those types of guys during her brief marriage. Yet Ethan was very down to earth.

"You're not the only one to laugh at my disdain for all things bugs. The guys in my squadron are forever giving me shit about it. If my canine partner could talk, I'm sure she'd tell me to suck it up. I swear I can cover myself with half a can of Off and they still manage to bite me."

Isabella walked over to Ethan and placed a hand on his arm. The heat from his skin immediately transferred to her hand, warming her blood. "I get the yard treated every month for mosquitos because, like you, I get eaten alive, but I also like to sit outside, and I won't let little bugs stop me from enjoying my backyard."

"Well, then, we can have a competition to see who will be the first one bitten."

Her lips stretched into a smile and she shook her head. How romantic were they, discussing bug bites?

But she wasn't supposed to be thinking anything romantic with Ethan. All day, she'd teetered on canceling because she didn't want to get involved with him. After this dinner, they would go their separate ways and never see each other again. They'd given it a chance and it hadn't worked out.

Keep telling yourself that, because deep down you know that's not true. You want to see where this connection leads.

The voice needed to go on a holiday somewhere far, far away, maybe Antarctica where internet and communication with the outside world was limited. Regardless of the truth of her inner thoughts, pursuing anything with Ethan would only end up in heartache—mainly hers.

She'd already lost one military man. She didn't want to lose another.

ETHAN PLACED HIS beer bottle on the glass-top table. Darkness had fallen and solar powered lights glowed among the flower beds.

The sound of a hand slapping flesh made him turn to Isabella. This was the fifth time she'd slapped away a bug. "I guess your blood is sweeter than mine."

"Shut up," she grumbled, but her smile suggested there was no malice in her words.

"I don't have a problem if you want to go inside. I know it's not my place, so I don't want to be presumptuous and all."

Her sigh sounded heavy in the still, night air. "The least the bugs can do is annoy you too."

Ethan threw his head back and laughed. "Oh no, trust me when I say I'm very glad I'm not being eaten."

"You know a real gentleman will tell the bugs to attack him first and not his companion."

"Are we really having this conversation?" he asked, enjoying every single second of it. He couldn't remember the last time he'd laughed so much.

"Well, it's a common enough type of conversation. Lots of people have issues with bugs, whether it's a fear of spiders or cockroaches. What would be nice tonight would be if the mosquitos didn't veer off the direction they were heading just to get a taste of my blood."

He didn't blame the bugs for wanting a taste of Isabella; after the short sample he'd had of her lips the previous evening and when he'd first arrived, there were plenty of places he'd like to discover if they were as sweet.

Now that was a conversation he didn't want to start—perhaps it was better to talk about night insects. Any topic was better than awkward silences between them.

"Summer vacation is a couple of months away. Do you have any plans?" he asked.

"Other than sleeping in beyond six a.m., nope, nothing planned at all. The break isn't really as long for a teacher as it is for the kids. I have to review lesson plans and adjust accordingly to any changes the district might make for the coming year."

"Does that happen often?"

"Pretty much every year. There's always changes to the way they'd like student assessments done. So I have to adjust my class plans to fit in those assessments while making sure my students absorb what I'm teaching them. Fifth grade is the big transition year for most kids."

"How so?" he asked. He'd never given much thought to what teachers had to go through year after year.

"Well, they're the 'seniors' of the elementary school, the leaders, you could say. I like the kids in my class to help out with the kindergarteners, read them stories. It's not always easy to get that to happen, but I've pushed for it over the last couple of years, and the relationships that have been generated between them are really sweet. There are always tears at the end of the year."

"I've never heard of that, but it's a cool idea. Quite a few guys on base have kids, and when we're deployed they're always getting letters from them, but there's never been anything mentioned along the lines of what you do. I remember fifth grade; some guys I knew would bully the younger kids. I often got into trouble because I'd confront them."

"It's one of the reasons I do it. It also gives the kids in third and fourth grade something to look forward to. I've had a couple of former fifth graders visit the school on their building's days off. They have lunch with the kids they've mentored. It really is a wonderful sight." She paused and gazed out into the darkness. "Dammit," she murmured.

"What's wrong?" he asked as he stood and scanned the backyard.

He'd been so lost in enjoying the moment with Isabella he hadn't been paying attention to his surroundings. Anyone could've jumped over the fence and attacked them. This was where he missed having Sam by his side—any potential threat and she'd growl in alert.

Fuck, this was the second time he'd lost his focus in Isabella's presence. The first being their disastrous blind date.

He was marching toward the dark corner of Isabella's yard when her hand landed on his arm. "Nothing, I just got bitten again. Maybe we should head inside."

The aroma of her wildflower scent wafted up to him, frying his senses once more. It was different to the one she'd worn the last couple of times they'd been together, and he liked it as much as her other perfume. He pulled her tight against him and looked down into her face. The glow from the patio lights highlighted her blonde hair. He brushed a stray strand behind her ear before closing the distance between them. Her lips had been tempting him ever since her kiss welcoming him into her house. His eyes drifted shut the second their lips connected.

Ethan tightened his grip around her waist and teased her mouth open with his tongue, allowing him to deepen the kiss. Her arms wound around his neck and their tongues dueled.

The kiss they'd shared last night was out of this world,

but nothing compared to the rush of sensations filling him now. Would it be so wrong to suggest they take this kiss into her bedroom? This was kind of their third date, and he couldn't deny how much he wanted to make love to Isabella. Kiss every inch of her skin. Find out what made her moan, and how she sounded when she came apart in his arms.

He needed air; he broke the kiss. He rested his forehead against hers, their ragged breathing sounding loud in the still, night air. "I've had a really good time tonight, Izzy."

"Me too," she replied, almost sounding surprised.

He filed that little tidbit away to look at later; right now, he didn't want to spoil the magic growing between them. He had an inkling her surprise was because she didn't want to enjoy spending time with him. Just like her dinner invitation the previous evening.

"I should go. I've got an early morning tomorrow."

"Tomorrow's Sunday though," she said, pulling out of his arms and going over to the table to collect their dessert plates.

"My team does PT every morning, come rain, hail, or shine. The earlier we do it, the less sting the sun has."

He followed her back into the house, hoping she'd ask him to stay, but he wasn't holding his breath. He placed the glasses he carried into the sink next to where she placed the plates. "Can I help you clean up?" he asked, another attempt to prolong the evening.

"Thanks, but no, I have it all under control."

Well, he didn't need to be told twice. That was a brush-off if he ever heard one. An awkwardness that had been missing all evening sprouted up between them. "Thanks for the invitation."

Geez, now that sounded really stilted.

Slim arms encircled his waist and instinct made him close his own around her warm body. "I had a nice time too, Ethan."

Ethan brushed his lips across the top of her hair. It was now or never. He had to take the plunge and see if Isabella was as invested in this as he was. "I'd like to see you again."

"I…uh."

Her hesitation killed him.

"Take a chance, Izzy. I promise you won't regret it." Damn, making promises was never a good idea. Some promises were impossible to keep, especially in his job. This one, however, he could keep without a doubt. No matter how long they had together, he would make sure she didn't ever regret taking a chance with him.

The silence stretched between them, and with every passing thump of his heartbeat, hope died a little more. It appeared they were destined to have only two and a half dates. If he was going to be rejected, he was going to take it like the warrior he was and never look back.

He pulled away and Isabella's beautiful blue eyes widened.

"Bye."

Chapter Seven

ETHAN CHECKED HIS uniform before he knocked on Lieutenant Colonel Shawn Blue's door. Being summoned to this office usually scared the shit out of Ethan, meant he'd fucked up on something. He didn't think he'd done anything, but his focus had been a bit scattered lately.

The abrupt way he'd walked out on Isabella after dinner at her place hadn't sat well with him. Yet she had accepted his apology, and they'd had a few fun, slightly flirty, text conversations. His last text was that he'd be in touch—that was five days ago.

He wanted to ask her out again, but hell, their track record for dates was abysmal. Why was he still trying?

Because you like her and want to get to know her better.

It was her hesitation when he asked about seeing her again that still confused him. At the time, he was sure she wanted to say yes, because her eyes had lit up when he asked her, but then dimmed.

Damn, he couldn't spend all day thinking. If he wanted to know the truth, he would have to ask her straight out rather than make assumptions. The question was, would she tell him when he asked?

Raising his hand, he rapped his knuckles against the wood. He needed to concentrate on this meeting. Never a good thing to get summoned to your commanding officer out of the blue.

"Enter."

Ethan walked in and nodded at his superior officer before standing, back ramrod straight, in front of the desk.

"Take a seat, Staff Sergeant Masters."

Ethan did as instructed, and waited for him to speak. The man seemed to enjoy dragging out the process, flicking through the papers on his desk before gathering them up and slipping them into a folder.

"How are things, Ethan?"

Okay, so it couldn't be too bad if Blue was calling Ethan by his first name. "I'm well and things are good, sir."

The other man picked up another file and opened it. "You've been with the 805th Security Forces Squadron a while now, haven't you?"

"Yes, sir." And he loved every single second of it. He couldn't imagine doing anything different.

"And you're scheduled to leave in just over a month for another stint overseas, correct?"

"Yes, sir, that's correct." The question seemed out of place considering the lieutenant colonel knew everything that went on around base. Well, at least he should.

Was his deployment being put off?

Was he being transferred to another squadron? He hoped not.

"When you return from your deployment, your reenlistment papers will come in."

Shit, he'd forgotten it was getting to that time again. Well, it was a no-brainer; he'd be signing up again for another go around.

What about Isabella?

No, the voice in his head didn't know what it was talking about. There was nothing going on between the two of them. Why would she even factor into his decision of whether he reenlisted or not?

"I'll admit, sir, that it slipped my mind."

"Have you considered what you might do in the future? You've been with the service for a while now."

What the hell? Does he think I want to retire?

This was a subject he wasn't expecting to discuss when he entered his commanding officer's office. Retirement for Ethan wasn't on the cards, not at least for another five years anyway, when he'd have completed twenty years of service. At that time, he didn't have to retire if he didn't want to.

"No, sir, I concentrate on the here and now."

His leader nodded and kept perusing the papers in front of him. This whole conversation seemed surreal. He had no idea what track his lieutenant colonel was walking down, but he hoped he'd find out soon.

"A position has become available that I want you to consider."

"What's that, sir?" Ethan sat a little straighter in his chair.

"Kennel master. You've got an impeccable record, and your commitment to the K-9 unit is second to none. This could be a Stripes for Exceptional Performers promotion. It's the next step in your career as well."

Definitely the last thing he was expecting when he walked into the office. It was an honor to be considered for the position, to know his hard work was recognized and it paid off. On the other hand, the thought of not being on the front line and helping his fellow airmen in his squadron was one he needed to get used to.

But the lieutenant colonel was still waiting for a response. "Thank you, sir, for believing me to be a suitable person to fill the role. It's a lot to consider."

The man leaned forward and clasped his fingers together on his desk. "You've been a handler for a while, so this is a natural progression for you in your career. It will also help you in whatever you decide to do after your time with us. Of course, it's a moot point if you decide not to reenlist. There would be no point going through the process of the promotion if you decided in six months' time you'd like to leave the service."

"Yes, sir, I agree. As I said it's a lot to think about." The walls seemed to be closing in on him. "Is that all, sir?"

"Yes, but seriously think about it, Masters. It will be

good for you."

Ethan stood, saluted his superior officer and walked out of the office. He closed the door and leaned back against the wall.

What the hell was he going to do?

NO, I WILL not check my phone.

Isabella kept chanting that line over and over in her mind as she sat in the staff room, eating her lunch. Five days had passed since her last text conversation with Ethan. How hard was it to send a how-are-you-doing text? It wasn't hard at all; anyone could do it.

Well, why haven't you?

Okay, yes, the voice was correct, she could've, and she'd picked up her phone a couple of times to do that. Except fear at putting herself out there had held her back. If he weren't so committed to his career, it would be a no-brainer. She'd be calling and texting him. Hell, if he weren't in the air force, she'd have leaped into his arms when he said he wanted to see her again.

"Oh, my God, if you glance at your phone once again, I'm going to throw it out the window," Meredith grumbled from across the table.

"I wasn't looking at it." Busted. She was totally gazing at her phone.

"Right, and I'm really the pope in disguise. Why don't you just pick up the phone and call or send him a text? It's not like you haven't made the first move before."

"He said he'd be in touch, so I'm waiting." Wow, that even sounded lame to her ears.

"Geez, Isabella, that's lame." The ability to practically read each other's minds was why they were best friends. They'd shared many secrets and ice cream over late-night marathon study sessions at Stephen F. Austin. In fact, it had been a while since they'd had one of those nights. Maybe they should do it again, and soon.

"We need to do an ice cream night." Isabella voiced her idea out loud. "What about Friday night?"

"What happens if GI Joe calls to arrange a date? Are you going to blow me off?"

Isabella almost choked on her sandwich. "What did you call him?"

Laughing, her friend tossed a potato chip in her direction. "You heard me. But I'm dead serious, I'm all for you dating, but I don't want to be blown off. That's not cool."

"Since when have I ever blown you off for a date?"

"Never," Meredith said on a shrug. "But there's always a first time for everything."

Isabella held up her right hand and covered her heart with it. "I, Isabella Knowles, do solemnly swear and declare that I will never blow off my best friend, Meredith Turner, after we make plans, no matter how awesome my date is or the event he has planned for us."

Another chip sailed in her direction, and this time Isabella caught it and popped it in her mouth.

"Well, that's going to the extreme, but I totally appreciate it."

"Good, now you do it to me."

Meredith rolled her eyes but repeated Isabella's words and actions.

"Good, now that's settled," Isabella said with a satisfied nod. "Friday night, ice cream, and binge watching a show to be determined upon your arrival."

"Sounds good."

A few minutes later Isabella's phone buzzed, signaling an incoming text.

Meredith laughed. "You know who that is, don't you?"

Well, she hoped she knew, but no way was she going to give Meredith the satisfaction of grabbing up her phone to confirm both their suspicions, no matter how much she wanted to do just that. "I have no idea."

"Oh, please stop. You totally want to snatch up your phone and read your message."

The phone buzzed again. Now it was getting hard to ignore. Isabella took another bite of her lunch, but her gaze kept darting to her phone.

"Oh, for goodness' sake, Iz, just pick up the damn phone." Meredith pushed the device toward her.

Sighing, she picked up the phone and her suspicions

were corrected—Ethan had texted her. Butterflies formed in her stomach and she wasn't sure she wanted to open the messages. Maybe he was giving her the brush-off. Maybe he was letting her know he was about to deploy.

Neither option appealed to her and he didn't seem the type of guy to break up, or send bad news through something as impersonal as a text message.

For crap's sake, she'd been independent since she made the decision to marry at eighteen. She thought of herself as a strong woman—the way she was acting over a couple of messages was really pathetic.

She picked up the phone and pulled up the message app.

"Hey, Izzy. Sorry I haven't contacted you, work has been crazy. Are you free Friday night?"

Of course, he'd want to make plans with her the second after she'd made plans with Meredith. It was always the way. Why couldn't he have said Saturday night?

"Is it GI Joe?" Meredith asked around a mouthful of her lunch.

Isabella rolled her eyes at her friend. "Yes, it's from Ethan. He wants to know if I'm free Friday night."

Meredith lowered her sandwich. "And?"

Meredith clearly expected her to cancel the plans they'd made five minutes ago. Only a selfish friend would ever ditch their girl after making arrangements. Never in her life had she backed out, and she wasn't planning to start now. "And

I'm going to tell him I have plans."

"You know you can change them if you want. I don't mind."

Another reason she loved Meredith—she was selfless. But Isabella missed spending time with her friend and she really did want to spend the night eating ice cream while watching romantic movies on Hallmark Channel. If Ethan was the type of guy she thought he was, he'd totally understand.

"I'm not breaking my word, Mere. I'm going to text Ethan and tell him I'm busy."

"I've already got plans Friday night with my friend, Meredith. I'm free Saturday."

Isabella hit send before she could second-guess herself. She placed the phone face down on the table beside her.

"Did you let him know you're free Saturday night? Because if you didn't, I may have to knock some sense into you."

Isabella laughed, her heart warming. "Yes, I told him I was free Saturday night."

Before she could say anything else, her phone buzzed again. This time she didn't dillydally.

"Saturday is out unfortunately. We have an overnight training exercise. Maybe next Friday?"

Training exercise.

Her heart pounded in her chest and a wave of heat flowed through her body. Travis had died at a training exercise. A rubber bullet struck his chest in between heartbeats, killing him. In a split second, the life she dreamed of was snatched away with a visit from the chaplain.

She couldn't do this again.

Maybe fate had been trying to protect her since the second she met Ethan. Why else would it seem like they went two steps forward and ten steps back?

"Iz, what is it? What's wrong? You look like you've seen a ghost."

"Nothing, it's nothing." But her voice shook.

Meredith stood, her chair scraping loudly across the floor. "Don't lie. Who sent you a text?"

"Ethan."

"Okay, what did he say that caused this reaction? Do I have to go deal with some stupid soldier ass?"

"Airman. He's air force, so he's an airman, not a soldier."

"Tomato. Tomahto. What's going on, Iz?"

Meredith knew about her past. She'd understand why Ethan's message triggered panic. Isabella looked at her friend, knowing the pain flowing through her was displayed in her eyes. "He can't meet me on Saturday because he's going on a training exercise."

Meredith's arms closed around her. They stayed like that for a few minutes. "It doesn't mean it's going to turn out the same way," her friend finally said. "I bet he's been on tons of training exercises and nothing's happened to him. You know what happened to Travis was a freak accident, right? You can't let the past hold you back from your future. Have a little fun. You've got nothing to lose."

After she'd emerged from the fog of mourning Travis's death and the death of her dream life, she'd vowed never again to get involved with a military man. Yet here she was, dating a man in the armed forces.

What Meredith said was true. What happened to Travis was a one-in-a-million occurrence, and Isabella should continue seeing Ethan because she enjoyed the banter they'd shared the last two times they'd been together, not to mention their text conversations. But her heart was begging her to run as far as she could to keep them both safe from shattering again.

Now was not the time to tempt fate, no matter how gorgeous Ethan Masters was.

Chapter Eight

TAPPING HIS FINGERS on his steering wheel, Ethan looked out the window at Isabella's house.

"I'm making a big mistake, aren't I, Sam?"

It wasn't normal to have his K-9 partner with him, but he'd sought permission to bring Sam home and Lieutenant Colonel Blue had allowed it. Anyone could've knocked him over with a squeaky toy when he'd received the affirmative. Ethan had quickly exited the office before Blue could change his mind.

Sam yipped behind him, no doubt telling him she was fed up with sitting in the back of the car.

"Okay, okay," he said beneath his breath, reached over to the seat beside him, and grabbed the bag of takeout Chinese and Sam's leash.

Turning up on Isabella's doorstep uninvited, with a bag of food and a dog, was like running into a gunfight without a gun. The chances this move would come back to bite him in the butt were huge, especially after the radio silence between them for the last week and a half.

He should cut and run. Except he never gave up on anything. There was a connection between him and Isabella, one he didn't want to ignore.

If she asked him to leave, he would, but he had to hear it from her.

Once Sam was clipped to her lead, he closed the car door and activated the alarm. The beep echoed around the quiet night. So much for surprising her.

"Let's go, Sam," he said quietly, and he and his partner wandered up the short path to the front door. His finger hovered over the doorbell, hesitating again. Sam nudged his leg; even she was impatient with his indecisiveness.

What was it about Isabella that made him act so out of character? Being this wishy-washy could get him killed when he and Sam were working. And wouldn't his teammates have a field day teasing him if they knew that, when he was around Isabella, he had the confidence of a piece of sand.

Ethan pressed the white round button. He tapped his fingers against his legs as he waited for her to answer the door. Sam sat obediently beside him, panting quietly into the night, until her ears perked up.

His grip tightened on the bag as the door opened.

"Ethan? Wh-what are you doing here?"

Holding up the bag, he pasted a smile on his face, ignoring the look of panic in her eyes. "Dinner?"

Wow, smooth, Masters, real smooth. That's certainly going to impress her.

He cleared his throat. "What I meant to say was *Hi, Isa-*

bella, I've brought you dinner."

She crossed her arms over her chest. "What if I've already eaten?"

Sam barked, drawing Isabella's gaze away from him, giving him a few seconds to get himself under control. It was make or break time. "You brought your dog? I didn't know you had a pet."

"Sam isn't my pet, she's my working partner. I work in the K-9 division in the air force."

"You can bring your working dog home with you each night? That's good."

Well, she might not have asked him in yet, but at least she was talking to him and the look of panic fading from her eyes. Bringing Sam was looking like a stroke of genius.

"No, working dogs stay on base."

"And yet, here you are with your dog." Her eyebrow rose, her arms dropped to her side, and a soft smile played across her lips.

"Let's just say I caught my lieutenant colonel on a good day. Can we come in?"

"Umm, sure." She stepped back and waved an arm. "Come on in."

Sam's nails clipped on the hardwood floor as they made their way down Isabella's hallway. He headed for the kitchen to put the food down. He'd dodged the first bullet. She hadn't had the door shut in his face. That would've been awkward.

"Dinner, huh? What culinary delights have you brought to tempt me with?"

"I've brought some Chinese," he said as he placed the bag on the kitchen counter.

"It smells good," she responded as she grabbed some plates from the cupboard.

"I went to the best place in San Antonio." He began to pull out the boxes. "I've got egg rolls, sweet and sour pork, Kung Pao chicken, Szechuan beef, fried rice, and steamed rice."

"Are there more people coming for dinner? Because that's a heck of a lot of food for two people. I imagine Sam won't be getting any."

Ethan chuckled. Yeah, he had gone overboard. "I wasn't sure what you liked so I wanted to cover all bases. And you're correct, Sam won't be getting any."

The dog let out a small whimper from her place on the floor. He looked at his K-9 partner and shook his head. She got plenty of treats and had a bowl of kibble before he left base; she shouldn't be hungry at all.

"Aww, that's not fair for Sam," Isabella murmured as she went to pat the dog, but she stopped before she touched her and straightened again. "Am I allowed to touch her?"

Ethan gave a hand signal, and the dog rose and nudged Isabella's hand. "She's off duty. You can pet her."

A smile stretched Isabella's lips wide and her blue eyes sparkled. She squatted down and started patting and cooing to his partner.

As much as he'd like to continue watching them getting to know each other, he transferred his attention back to the food. The plan he'd come up with when he'd made the decision to get Sam for the night, was to find out once and for all if they had a future together. Sam was doing exactly what he hoped she would, breaking the ice between them.

"Your Sam really is beautiful," Isabella said.

"She's a good dog. I would be lost without her."

The scent of wildflowers wafted around him as Isabella came to stand beside him. "How long have you two been a team?"

"Three years. She's my second dog. My first one was getting close to retirement age. Violet was a great dog as well, and I think she taught me more than I ever thought a dog could."

"How so?" Isabella asked as she began heaping her plate with a combination of the chicken and sweet and sour dish. Another point on his side—he'd picked food she liked.

Ethan grabbed a plate and followed suit. Once they were seated, he picked up the conversation. "I was just out of training and, like all rookies, I believed I was untouchable. I thought I knew everything about being a K-9 handler, as I'd been in security forces since I enlisted, just another squadron. We were in a training exercise, and no matter how many times my trainer told me to trust in Violet, I still believed I knew everything."

"That's, um, bad."

"Tell me about it. Anyway, one of the devices was smoking when it shouldn't have been. If Violet hadn't pushed me in the opposite direction, we would've been in the direct line of fire when it exploded. From that second on, I didn't second-guess her when her behavior changed. I learned my lesson. The dog is always right. It's our job to go into buildings first. Sam's job is to sniff out any hidden dangers, and I report back to the team. If I don't trust my partner, it could end up in a disaster."

Isabella's fork clattered to her plate.

Fuck, why do I always mention how dangerous my job is?

He couldn't avoid talking about his job though; it was who he was. Getting Isabella off side wasn't going to help him with his real mission tonight.

Ethan reached over the table and laid a hand over hers. "It was one time and, as you can see, I'm still here."

She pushed away from the table, as though she wanted to get as far away from him as possible.

"I think you should go. Thank you for bringing me dinner." She was out of the kitchen before he could even stand up.

Shit, he'd well and truly fucked things up.

Was pursuing Isabella really worth all this pain?

Yes.

His job was always about protecting people and the guys in his team. He wanted to protect Isabella. She was hurting, and he needed to know why so he could fix it. If, in the end, walking away was what she needed him to do, he would. But only after they'd really talked. Laid everything out on the table. Plus, his attraction for her wasn't dying; it was getting stronger with every second he spent with her.

Without knowing all the facts, he was riding blind. Nothing ever good came of not seeing where you were going.

Sam trotted down the hallway behind Isabella and Ethan stared at his partner. Never before had Sam gone off on her own, especially not without a command from him. What was his dog doing?

He followed his dog, attempting to get his thoughts in order. He needed to fix this situation and fast.

As he reached the living room he stopped dead. Isabella was sitting on the couch. Sam had jumped up beside her and laid her head in Isabella's lap. Isabella, in turn, was running a hand down her back in an automatic motion as if this were a normal, everyday occurrence. Offering comfort wasn't a usual action for a K-9 dog; there were service dogs who did that for victims.

He wandered into the room and squatted down in front of Isabella, laying a tentative hand on her knee. She didn't brush him off; he took it as a good sign.

"I'm sorry, Izzy. I didn't mean to scare you." Keeping his voice low and modulated, he added, "I keep saying the wrong thing when I'm around you. It was never my intention to come here tonight and tell you about my close calls."

NICOLE FLOCKTON

"I know, but it's the reality of your job, isn't it? I'm not sure I can do this, Ethan."

Sam raised her head at that moment and looked directly at Ethan, her silent message clear. *Fix this problem, you need her.* How a dog could tell what he did and didn't need was beyond Ethan's understanding, but he wasn't going to ignore the silent edict. They were a team, he and Sam; he trusted his life with her and vice versa. Reaching out, he scratched her between the ears, her favorite spot. A soft sigh rippled out of the dog.

"Izzy, look at me." He waited until she turned to face him. The light had dulled in her eyes. He wanted to kiss her so badly. Kiss her until the fear and sadness was replaced with lust and desire. Yet that would be the same as putting a Band-Aid over a cut that needed stitches. After a while, the Band-Aid would fall off and the wound would weep until it became infected. The last thing he wanted was to infect this burgeoning relationship between him and Isabella.

"I realize that we've only been on a couple of dates, but I can't deny that I really like you and want to spend time with you. I also understand that my job is a big chasm between us. You told me you don't date military guys, but you called me after our aborted blind date. All I'm asking is for you to talk to me. Tell me what's going on in your mind. Help me understand you better."

In reality, Ethan had no idea if things between him and Isabella would work out for the long haul. There were no guarantees in life, especially with his job. Perhaps the best thing would be to walk away. Cut the ties before they became too ingrained in him.

Her lack of words told him what he needed to know. Quitting them was the right thing to do. The hurt would last only a short while, so better to do it now before either one of them got hurt even more.

He leaned over and placed a kiss on her cheek. "Actually, maybe you're right. Maybe this isn't the best thing for both of us. I'm sorry to disturb your evening. I wish you a beautiful life, Isabella Knowles. You deserve nothing less."

THE LETTERS ON the page in front of Isabella blurred yet again. How had last night turned into such a disaster quicker than a kindergartner on his first day streaking past his teacher to get one last hug from his mom?

"Who died?"

Isabella looked up and saw Meredith standing in the hallway. Thank goodness she'd had cafeteria duty and hadn't been able to have lunch with her friend. No way could she hide her feelings from eagle-eyed Meredith, hence this opening salvo.

She pointed her pen at the paper in front of her. "Katie's poor attempt at telling a story. I swear she copied her sister's work from two years ago."

Meredith sauntered into the room and plopped down in the chair on the opposite side of Isabella's desk. "Nice try, but I'm not buying it. I was standing at the door for a good five minutes, and let me tell you, you weren't reading a word on that page. So again, who died?"

Damn, sometimes working with her best friend really was the pits. Maybe she could fob her off with a little white lie. "Nothing, just tired. I couldn't sleep last night," she said as she put a hand beneath her desk and crossed her fingers.

A speculative gleam entered Meredith's eyes. Uh-oh, had she made the situation worse? "Ohhh, did GI Joe come a knocking and keep you up late? Spill the goods, girl."

Isabella laughed despite herself. Trust Meredith to take a lie and run with it full steam. Pretending she'd slept with Ethan was definitely better than having to explain everything to Meredith, but lying to her friend left a bad taste in her mouth.

"Not quite. I think that ship has sailed."

"I thought he was air force, not navy."

"Yes, but what's that got to do with it?" she asked.

"Well, instead of the ship has sailed, you need to say you crashed and burned. Or did *he* crash and burn? Could he not get it up?"

Isabella picked up her eraser and tossed it at her friend. "I don't know if you're insulting me or him. But no." She sighed. Maybe talking to Meredith would help her settle everything in her mind. "Mere, I just can't get over the fact he's in the military."

"Still? I thought we'd worked that out. Didn't we decide that you were going to have a little fun with him?"

"Well, yeah, but he surprised me last night with dinner and his working dog, Sam."

"Aww, that's sweet. So what happened that you have the look you're only supposed to have when your best friend deserts you, which, obviously, I haven't?"

Isabella rolled her eyes. Meredith thought very highly of herself. "He told me about his first dog, Violet, and how she pushed him out of the way during a training exercise when a device accidentally started smoking."

Meredith studied her for a few moments, canting her head to the side. "And you immediately went to Travis and what happened to him, so you shut yourself down without any explanation."

Yep, her friend had the uncanny knack of hitting the nail on the head with more accuracy than a carpenter.

"Yes." Really, there was no point denying it. Talking it out was what she needed to do and who better than her friend?

"How many times do I have to tell you…" Meredith stood and leaned over the desk as far as she could. "It. Was. A. Freak. Accident. What happened to Travis isn't going to happen to Ethan or anyone else."

"I know you're right. But, emotionally, it scares me so much. Ethan told me last night that he and his dog are first into buildings. He puts himself in danger every single time."

"How long has he been in the service?"

Isabella paused. "I think since high school. He told me his whole family is military. He's always known what he wanted to do."

"Okay, so he's been deployed a few times then, correct?"

"I guess so."

"Look, Iz, I love you; you're my best friend. The past has you chained so firmly in the here and now because it feels safe. You don't have to take a risk. I'm going to ask you something I've never asked you before. If the roles had been reversed and you'd died in a freak accident, would you expect Travis to let your death overshadow the rest of his life?"

"Of course not." The words burst out of her without hesitation.

Shit. She would be angry if Travis shut himself away like she had over the last ten years. She'd been fooling herself for so long, but she still didn't know which way to go. She couldn't totally leave Travis and their romance behind. But facing her past and pursing this attraction with Ethan would put her heart at risk again. Could she do it?

"You're right," she murmured before turning to see her friend a couple of feet away from her. "I have to think about which way I want to handle things, but you're right—again."

"Of course I am," Meredith responded with a big, cheeky grin. "So, here's another piece of advice. Call GI Joe.

You know you want to. You've been miserable all day, haven't you?"

"Yes. Which is stupid as I hardly know the guy."

"But you're attracted to him. Hell, girl, take a chance for once in your life. Even when you were with that bank manager you were seeing for a couple of months, the dreamy look that enters your eyes when you talk about Ethan was never there. I get that the thought of him being in the military scares you, but I'm tired of having this conversation with you. If you don't take the plunge, I'm not going to be your friend anymore."

"Dramatic much?"

Meredith shrugged. "Whatever. I'll do whatever I have to do to get you to start living and having fun. And if something happens, I'm only a phone call away—always, so don't forget that."

Isabella closed the distance between them and wrapped her friend in a hug. "Thank you for always kicking me in the butt when I need it."

"If you listened to me in the first place, I wouldn't have to keep doing it." But her friend tightened her arms. There was nothing like a Meredith hug. A second later, the hug was over. "Now, go call that man, apologize, and explain your past. You may be surprised at what happens. As a conversation breaker, tell him you're on your period and you're overemotional."

Isabella rolled her eyes and laughed. "Ew, gross. No way

am I going to say that to him. But, yeah, I need to tell him about Travis. If I put aside his career, there's a connection between me and Ethan. Our dates haven't been the best, but they've been fun. I've felt energized after our interactions in a way I haven't felt in years."

"I'm glad to hear it. It's about time you looked forward instead of backward." Meredith headed out the door, pausing to look back at her. "I expect you to call me and give me all the details."

"Fine. And, Mere?"

"Yeah?"

"Thanks. I don't know what I'd do without you."

"You'd be fine, but I'm banking some favors for whenever I need you."

With a wave, her friend walked out the door. Meredith was the strongest woman Isabella knew, but if her bestie ever did need Isabella, she'd be there for her—without fail.

Collecting her things, she'd grade the papers at home after she'd called Ethan, Isabella walked out of her classroom emotionally lighter than when she'd walked into it eight hours ago.

Chapter Nine

THE RHYTHMIC POUNDING of his shoes as they hit the pavement did nothing to soothe the riot of emotions running through Ethan. Over the years, he'd never thought of himself as an emotional guy. Hell, the lives of many men depended on him keeping his cool. Sam and he were nearly always the first into situations, sniffing out buildings for explosives as well as the scent of the person they were chasing.

As he rounded the corner of his street his phone buzzed, cutting off Jon Bon Jovi mid-lyric. The desire to let the phone go to voicemail was huge, but his training was too ingrained. Ignoring a call wasn't done in the military. It wasn't like he was on a special forces team that got calls and had to go wheels up in less than an hour, but still, sometimes they were called out on emergencies to help the local law enforcement.

The chances of it being Isabella were unlikely. That plane had well and truly flown over the horizon.

Fuck, he'd been doing so well, it had only been a half an hour since he last thought of her. How many mistakes had he made today because of his distraction? Too many to count, and Lieutenant Colonel Blue had been less than impressed, making Ethan do countless push-ups and crunches.

Slowing to a jog, he pulled his phone out of the pocket of his arm strap, almost dropping it when he saw Isabella's name flash across the screen. He shook his head convinced he was imaging her name. But, no, there it was, still flashing and if he didn't answer it soon, he'd most likely miss the call.

"Isabella, is everything okay?"

"Hi, and no, everything is not okay."

Immediately he went on high alert. "What's wrong? Are you in danger? Have you called 9-1-1? Don't move. Give me your coordinates and I'll be right there."

If she was in danger, he was going to go all airman on her.

"I'm at home and I'm not in any danger. No need to get all bossy on me."

"Well, then, don't call me and tell me everything's not okay. I can't help going into action mode, it's what I'm trained to do. I'm not going to apologize for it."

He was in the air force. If Isabella couldn't accept that then there really was no future for them. Hadn't that been the reason he'd walked out of her place the previous evening?

Her sigh echoed down the line and, even though he was annoyed with her and had convinced himself whatever they had was over, his body immediately responded to the sound.

"Ethan, I'm sorry. I didn't call to fight. I called because…"

Silence stretched between them and he began to walk back to his house. Thank goodness he wasn't too far away when Isabella called, he didn't think he'd be able to get his rhythm back again. "Because?" he prompted.

"I want to see you. Can you come over to my place? Or I can come to yours if that works better."

His heart rate increased again, and it wasn't from him picking up his pace to get home faster. "Umm, I'm just out running, but I should be home in about ten minutes. I can be at your place in…"—he looked at his watch and did a mental calculation—"forty-five minutes. Will that work?"

"Yeah, that will be great. Thanks, Ethan, I'll see you soon."

The call disconnected before he had a chance to respond. Picking up his pace again, he jogged toward his house, his step much lighter than it had been ten minutes ago.

TWENTY-FOUR HOURS AGO Ethan had found himself in the exact same position he was currently in—standing out front of Isabella's door—and he'd bombed out, believing whatever they had was over. This time he'd been invited.

Before he could depress the button signaling his arrival, the door was pulled open. His breath caught at the sight in front of him. Isabella was wearing a long dress that wasn't clingy but hinted at the delectable delights beneath. Her bare feet were sticking out from beneath the soft fabric. She looked so cool and casual.

"Hi." The word rushed out of him.

"Hey, thanks for coming over. I realize it's a little late. Come in." She stepped back, and like the previous evening he preceded her down the hallway. Unlike the previous evening, he didn't wander into the kitchen but waited until she had secured the front door and joined him.

"Why don't we sit outside, it's a nice evening."

"Sure. Sounds good."

Nerves sizzled through his bloodstream, an emotion he was getting used to experiencing around Isabella.

"Take a seat I'll be back in a second."

Isabella rushed back into the house while he walked over to the small table they'd sat at the first time he was at her house. The night where she'd cooked, and they'd had a wonderful time.

A few moments later she returned with a plate of cookies, the scent of cinnamon and chocolate wafted toward him. "Did you make these?" he asked as he reached for one of the still warm cookies.

"Yes, I did. Well me and a roll of cookie dough I had in the refrigerator." She indicated to the pitcher of tea on the table. "Would you like a drink?"

"Thanks, that'd be great." What he'd really like would be

for her to get down to why she'd asked him over. As she said, it wasn't exactly early and five a.m. was going to come around pretty quickly.

Once she'd placed the glass in front of him and he'd eaten another cookie, he noticed her straightening in her chair, as if preparing herself to get down to why they were currently sitting opposite each other.

"Ethan, I want to apologize for the way I acted last night after you shared what happened with your first dog with me." The words tumbled out of her mouth like a new puppy who tripped over his paws while trying to work out how to run and walk.

"No apologies necessary. I should've watched what I said. I know that you're still not used to the idea of my occupation." And he would love to understand why that was. Honestly, it was something he should've asked her on their second date.

"That's the thing, you shouldn't have to watch your words around me. It's not fair to you. It's my issue and I have to deal with it."

"How about sharing it with me and then we can deal with it together?"

"It's complicated," she started and then stopped.

"Isn't everything in life?"

She chuckled softly. "Yeah, you're right. You know my dad was in the military, did I tell you that?"

Her father was in the military, and she had a problem

with it? What the hell?

Years of training to expect the unexpected enabled him to keep his expression neutral. "No, I didn't know that."

"Yeah, he goes down to the veterans' center and plays cards with the guys. One day a grandson of his friend happened to be there. Dad started talking about me and the next thing I know Dad's calling me telling me about this date he'd set me up on."

The more she talked, the more everything fell into place. Ethan was well aware that Linc would go play cards with his grandfather. "That would be Linc you're talking about. I'm pretty sure at the time of the *arrangement*, I wasn't in on the agreement. I went out one night with Linc and, well, let's just say the next time he dares me to a drinking game, I'm going to be saying no."

Isabella laughed. "Well, it hasn't turned out so bad, has it?"

Ethan raised his eyebrow, she really didn't think their false starts were a bad thing? "I don't know, you tell me. You know I've been more than happy to see you, it's you who's been throwing up the barriers."

A little of the lightness shining in her eyes dimmed. He steeled himself from feeling guilty. They'd been playing this back and forth game for a few of weeks now. The time had come to go forward or stick to his guns and not at all.

"This is true," she said quietly and took a sip of her drink.

He wondered if she was taking the time to collect her thoughts. There was no way she was getting ready to tell him to leave and never come back. If she'd felt that way, she wouldn't have called him.

"What's going on here, Izzy? You're sending so many mixed signals I don't know which ones to read. If we are to move forward you're gonna need to start talking. Explain why you asked me over. As nice as the cookies are, I'm sure your invite wasn't for a late evening tea party."

A shudder rippled through her body. "God, I really don't know where to start. Every time I think I've got it sorted in my brain, I open my mouth to speak and then nothing comes out."

"I think the beginning really is when you told me your dad was in the military. Which branch?"

"Army. Like you, I'm the quintessential military brat, moving from base to base. Never staying long enough to form lasting friendships."

Yeah, it was tough way to grow up, but he'd been lucky. He had grown up on different bases, but he'd had a more settled childhood than most kids. His mom handled each move with a smile. Still, he suspected there was more to Isabella's story than she was letting on.

"How long did your dad serve?" he asked.

"He did his twenty and then did a few more. He works part-time at one of the large hardware stores. I suspect he'll go full-time soon. He moved to San Antonio when I settled here a couple years ago." She sighed and picked at the fabric of her dress. "Our relationship has many ups and downs, it always has. He went on a trip just after our second date and I haven't spoken to him about it since he returned."

"What about your mom?" he asked. Thinking back over their dates, not once had she mentioned her mom.

"I don't know where she is. I haven't seen her since she walked out on me and Dad when I was a teenager."

Shit, that had to be the hardest thing for a girl to grow up with—no mother figure. "I'm sorry, Izzy."

She shrugged off his sympathy. "It was a long time ago and, after she left, Dad worked hard to get on a special forces team so we had some sort of stability and didn't have to move around so much."

"I wouldn't have thought that was a good type of stability. Usually those guys are sent into situations that are far more dangerous than what I see when I'm deployed."

"You're right, it wasn't pleasant when he went away, but as I said, it was far better than what we had both been living with for countless years."

There was so much more to this story and he wished Isabella would just spill it. "What were you living with, Izzy?"

"My parents fought all the time. Mom hated military life, which was dumb because Dad was in the army when they'd met. I'd go into my room and shove my head under a pillow so I didn't have to hear the ugly words my mom spewed at Dad. It was worse when Mom decided to hit the bottle. Things always turned ugly then."

No girl, or son for that matter, should be exposed to what she had been exposed to. Unfortunately, it wasn't an uncommon story in military or civilian life. A guy at his school had had to deal with a deadbeat father while his mom worked three jobs to keep food on the table. It hadn't worked out well for that family; all three had died in a car accident—his father was driving when he shouldn't have been. "Saying sorry that you had to go through that seems so pitiful, but it's true. I wish things could've been different for you."

He was also slowly beginning to understand her aversion to being with someone in the military. "I'm guessing your mom didn't deal well when your dad was deployed."

A harsh laugh erupted out of her. "That's an understatement. Mom would disappear for the first couple of days."

"What about the other women from the base? Or your dad's unit? Did no one help you?"

"Oh, yeah, they were great. They would feed me and say I could stay there, but I'd always go back home, just in case. When Mom returned, we both acted as if nothing had happened. I never asked where she went because I never wanted to know. When I got married, I was determined to be completely different from her. I couldn't wait to experience the real joys of being a proud wife of my military man, like some of the women I saw on base."

"You're married?" He glanced at her left hand and

couldn't see a ring. Nothing in her house suggested she had a significant other in her life. Was her breakup recent? Was that why her dad set her up on a blind date?

"Was. I'm a wi-widower." Her voice broke.

And, as if a lightbulb turned on above his head, everything fell into place.

He stood and went over to where she sat. The devastation in her eyes when she looked up at him pierced him in the middle of his chest. He held out his hand, not saying anything just hoping she'd reach out to him. When her smaller hand slid into his, he smiled softly and tugged so she was standing next to him. Wrapping his arms around her, he pulled her tightly against his chest, relishing the feel of her in his arms again. They stood there for a few seconds before he walked them over to the small couch on her patio.

He took hold of her hand, blowing out a short breath when she didn't snatch it away. "I'm sorry, Izzy. So sorry that you had to go through that. Can you tell me what happened? I'm assuming he died in action?"

Another shudder rippled through her but her stiff body relaxed at the end of it. "Travis and I were high school sweethearts. With Dad based in Fort Hood, I was able to enjoy my final years of high school. Get involved with all the activities. I wasn't popular, but I was a damn good band leader. Travis was on the football team, one of the stars, and had the cheerleaders fighting to get his attention. He ignored them and zeroed in on me. We were inseparable after our first movie date.

"Travis, like you, knew he wanted to go into the army the second he finished high school, and he asked me to marry him on graduation day. I said yes because all I'd dreamed about was being his wife and supporting him with his career. A month later, we were married at city hall."

A million thoughts swirled around Ethan's brain. Her voice had softened as she spoke about her husband, her love for him obvious.

"What did your dad think of your marriage?"

Isabella sighed, her thumb making random patterns on the top of his hand. "Dad wasn't happy at all. He wanted me to go to college and do the long-distance thing. But I just wanted to be a wife and a mom as soon as possible. When he could see I was determined to do it, not to mention how happy I was, he gave his blessing. Dad liked Travis and had no doubts that he would look after me."

"Did your husband die on deployment?"

Her breath hitched, and she closed her eyes momentarily. When she opened them they glistened with unshed tears. Fuck, this wasn't going to be good.

"No, he died here in the States during a training exercise."

Jesus, no wonder she freaked when he told her about his close call. The memories it must have brought up for her. "What happened to him?"

"A rubber bullet hit him in the chest between heartbeats

and he died. They tried CPR, but it didn't work. It's the sort of accident that's more than likely going to happen to an adolescent than adult. One minute he was there, the next he was gone. I hadn't spoken to him for a week. I never got a chance to say goodbye."

Her hands covered her face as the tears tracked down her cheeks. He gathered her close and rubbed circles across her back. Every word about her husband stuck a dagger deeper and deeper inside of him. Her admiration and love for the fallen soldier was palpable—how could he compete with that?

HOW COULD BEING held by Ethan feel so right after talking about the man she'd promised to love for eternity when she was eighteen? It was hard to relive the memories of the short time she had with Travis and the circumstances of his death. The flag they'd given her from his coffin was in a box on the top shelf of her closet. She couldn't bear to have it on display at the time. After a while, it seemed easier to keep it there. Being with Ethan resurrected memories she thought she'd dealt with. How wrong she'd been. Instead of living, she'd been existing.

"I'm sorry, Izzy. So, so sorry." The pain in Ethan's voice echoed hers.

"Thank you." What more could she say? Yes, talking

about Travis had been difficult, but, right now, she felt as if part of the binds that had been shackling her were finally breaking free.

Being in Ethan's arms was giving her the courage to believe she could be strong enough to deal with being in a relationship with a military man.

He released her from his hold and stood. A chill swept over her at the loss of his warmth. "I think it would be best if I leave. I'm bringing up too many memories, and I don't want to cause you any more pain." He leaned down and kissed her softly on the forehead. "I hope you find someone who makes you as happy as Travis did."

For a heartbeat she sat, shocked at his departure. He was at the French doors when she sprang up. "Wait, Ethan." He paused but didn't turn.

She could let him walk through the door and out of her life, permanently. Or she could take the leap. The leap her dad called her a coward for not taking. The leap she needed to start to truly live her life again.

"I don't want you to go," she said. "I want you to stay."

Ethan turned, his face partially in the shadows so she couldn't read his expression. "Are you sure? Because we've been doing this forward and backward dance since we met."

No truer words had been spoken. The dance they'd been doing was mainly because she was leading it. Leading it in the wrong direction.

Isabella joined him by the door. "I'm very sure, Ethan. I

told you about Travis because you need to know where I come from and what I've been through. I'm only now working out that I do want to live and take risks." She reached out and placed her hand on his arm. An electric current hummed between them, and Ethan's muscle jerked beneath her fingers. "I want to take that risk with you, Ethan. Will you take it with me?"

She held her breath, waiting for his answer. His eyes were shuttered from her and his body rigid beside her.

"Are you sure, Izzy?" he asked.

God, every time he called her Izzy a thrill buzzed through her bloodstream. The frozen wall around her heart was beginning to melt a little. "Yes, I'm sure."

He hooked a finger under her chin and nudged it up so she was looking at him. God, he was so handsome. His features were accentuated in the dim backyard lighting. Shadows enhanced the strong line of his jaw. His pupils dilated when she reached up and placed her hand against his cheek, the roughness of his five-o'clock shadow pricking her palm.

"I can't fight my feelings for you anymore, Izzy?" he said in a whisper.

"I can't either," she responded before she moved so she could place her lips over his.

Ethan's arm swept around her back and lifted her so he could deepen the kiss. His tongue traced the seam of her lips encouraging her to open up and she did. Her own arms moved up and around his shoulders, her fingers cupping the back of his head, letting him know the last thing she wanted was for their kiss to end.

This was what she'd been craving for so long. To be held in the arms of a man again. A man who was good and kind, and Ethan was all that. He might not be Travis, but it didn't matter.

God, the man could kiss. Never had she been swept away by a simple kiss like this. Nothing mattered except being held by him. Not what would happen when he went away on a training exercise or deployment. All that mattered was for this moment in time it was just the two of them sharing something special.

She gasped in a lungful of air as he trailed his mouth along her jaw, alternating between nipping at her tender flesh and then soothing the little bites with his tongue and lips. Heat pooled between her thighs and she shifted in an attempt to alleviate the growing desire in her. If anything, it only heightened her need for him.

"God, Ethan, I want you." Her eyes snapped open the second the truth of her words hit her. She did want Ethan.

He chuckled against her neck and an involuntary shiver wracked her body. "I want you too, Izzy. And as much as I'd like to continue this inside, I think we probably need to slow things down. Take our time. We're beginning all over again."

Her head dropped to his shoulder, inhaling his scent, a mixture of spice and lemon. A scent she could easily get addicted to, and she'd be totally fine getting addicted to Ethan. "You're right, but I can be a little unhappy about it."

"I am, too, but I want to do things the right way," he murmured as he ran his hand up and down her back, keeping her firmly entrenched in post kiss bliss. "What are you doing on Saturday?"

"Nothing. Why?"

"One of the guys is having a grill-out and I was wondering if you wanted to come along?"

"You want me to meet your friends?" It was one thing to wrap her mind around pursuing a relationship with Ethan. It was another to meet his friends and immerse herself in a world that had been snatched away from her.

"Yeah, I do. And, after what you told me, I know inside you're freaking out a little."

"I'm not sure, Ethan. We've only just agreed to move forward with seeing each other. Meeting the guys you work with, and their partners, is a big step. Are we ready for that?"

"I'm sure it will be hard." He brushed a finger down her cheek. "But, yes, this is a new start for us and I want to share my military family with you. You won't have to do it alone; I'll be right beside you every step of the way. Please say yes."

How could she deny him his request when he'd been patient and understanding with her during their stop/start beginning? She'd asked him over tonight for a purpose—to move forward. The only way to find out if she was cut out for a relationship between them was to close her eyes and jump.

Chapter Ten

THE PHONE RINGING on the table had her heart leaping out of her chest. "I seriously have to get over myself," she mumbled as she reached for her phone.

Her initial instinct was to ignore the call when she saw *Dad* flashing on the screen. After her talk with Ethan the other night, she'd become aware that for her to move on with her life she also needed to talk to her dad about their relationship, only she hadn't summoned up the courage to phone him. She wanted her dad in her life. What girl didn't? Fathers were the ultimate champions, but she'd never let her dad be her champion. She'd been thirteen and hormonal when Mom had left them. Everything was changing in her life and she didn't have her mom to guide her through all the changes. With usual teenage irrational anger, she'd blamed Dad and his job for everything going wrong.

Now, through the wisdom of an adult, nothing her dad could've done would've made her mom happy.

Just like she was building a relationship with Ethan, re-building her relationship with her father was a priority too. After all, if it weren't for Dad, she wouldn't be getting ready to go out with Ethan today.

"Hey, Dad, how are you? How was your trip?"

"Hey, honey bee, I'm good and the trip was great. Got some deer and boar. I'll bring you over some meat if you'd like."

Honey bee? Why was he calling her by the name he hadn't used in years? After their last conversation when he dared her to call Ethan, she'd expected him to be short and crisp with her.

His meat offer wasn't new; he always gave her that option whenever he returned from his trips, and every time she said no. It wasn't that she didn't like the meat, when he hadn't been deployed he'd gone hunting and she'd been more than happy to eat her fair share of what he'd caught.

If she thought about it, those times were good when he'd grill the meat and she'd sit outside and talk to him. Most of those times had happened when she'd been in high school. After Mom left, he had always made sure he was around and if he had to go away, he ensured she was looked after. Hmm, she'd forgotten about June, the lady who looked after her. June had been a shoulder to cry on when the kids at school played a prank on Isabella. Had helped her understand that, in life, there were always people who would do things she didn't agree with.

How could she have forgotten June?

"Isabella, are you still there?"

"Yeah, Dad, sorry I was thinking about June."

"Oh, yes, she was wonderful, God rest her soul."

Isabella sat a little straighter in her chair. "She's dead?"

"Yeah, she died last year of a heart attack. I thought I told you?"

"I don't think you did. Or if you did I didn't pay attention to what you were saying." Her voice trailed off and sorrow slammed into her like a freight train. How selfish had she become? So consumed in her determination to ignore everything about her past that she forgot about the woman who tried to make her feel comfortable in an uncomfortable situation.

"I'm sorry, honey bee, I haven't been the best in keeping communication lines open with you."

She shook her head, even though her dad couldn't see her. "No, it's not your fault, Dad. I need to take some responsibility as well. I haven't exactly been forthright in talking to you either."

"Guess we both should try and do a little better, huh?"

"Yeah, Dad, we should. Let's get together tomorrow and I'll come and get some of the meat you offered, if that's okay."

"I'd love that. There's enough here to feed an army." He chortled at his own joke and Isabella joined it. It had been a long time since she and her dad had connected. "And speaking of army, did you take up my dare? Did you hit it out of the park, or did you strike out?"

Baseball? "Since when did you start using baseball analogies?"

"Oh, Jerry used them. I guess some of them stuck in my mind."

Again she shook her head, enjoying the lightness in her father's voice. Seemed like he'd done some thinking about their relationship, too, while he was away. "Right, well, please don't, I can't take all these changes at once."

"Changes? What changes are you talking about?" This was a serious dad tone. "Do I need to go do some recon and take him out?"

A knock at the door pulled her attention from her dad's attempt at a threat. "No, Dad, you don't need to do that," she started as she got up and walked to the front door. "In fact, Ethan just knocked on my door. We're going out today."

"Is that right? Well, I guess Dad did knock it out of the park. So things are going well?"

She opened the door and pointed to the phone. She also made sure she kept eye contact with Ethan as she answered her dad's question. "Yes, Dad, things are going well, now. We hit a few bumps, but Ethan's a good guy."

A large smile broke out over her face when she glimpsed a faint pink hue bloom over Ethan's cheeks. She never took him as one to be embarrassed easily. Especially not considering the way they'd met.

"Well, I'm glad it worked out. I won't keep you any longer, but bring him over tomorrow. I want to meet this young man."

"I'll check to see if he's free, Dad."

"Hmph, if he can't make time to meet your dad, then he's not worth it," he grumped over the phone. Hearing her dad become all protective over a guy again made her smile grow bigger.

"I'll send you a text later and let you know. Bye, Dad."

"Bye, honey bee."

She ended the call, and looked up to find Ethan watching her intently. "I take it I've been summoned to meet your dad?"

Nerves about the approaching get-together jangled to life and began clattering about in her tummy. There was nothing in his tone to suggest he was freaked out by the idea or was unhappy with it. "Umm, yeah. How do you feel about that?"

Ethan shrugged and then leaned forward to kiss her softly on the lips. "I'll be happy to meet your dad, Izzy."

Relief swept through her and she gripped the door to stop herself from falling. "You know he'll probably grill you?" she said as she walked into her house, knowing Ethan was going to follow her.

"I would expect nothing less. Do I need to wear my dress uniform? Do you think that will impress him?"

"I don't know about impressing Dad, but it would impress the hell out of me," she murmured. The image of Ethan dressed in his formal uniform made her weak at the knees. She'd always been a sucker for a man in uniform.

Arms slipped around her waist as warm lips landed on her bare shoulder. She shivered at the contact, her eyes drifting shut, and she allowed her body to relax against Ethan's strong one.

"Anytime you want me to wear my dress blues I will." He turned her in his arms and the lips that had been creating havoc on her shoulder crashed down on hers.

This.

This was what she'd been dreaming about since he'd left two nights ago. She floated through work Friday and Meredith had taken one look at her and gave her a high five. The soft fabric of Ethan's shirt did nothing to hide the warmth emanating from him. A warmth that enveloped her like his embrace, making her feel content. Something she hadn't felt in a long time.

Reluctantly, he pulled his lips away from hers. His chest moved up and down rapidly beneath her fingers. Hers danced in time with him. Their bodies were tightly aligned and she couldn't mistake the effect their kiss had on a certain part of him.

A wave of mischief trickled through the desire strumming in her veins, and she swiveled her hips against him. She was rewarded with a groan. "We have a party to get to. Don't tempt me into brushing it aside and staying here."

"I wouldn't mind," she said as she repeated her action.

This time his lips landed on hers and his own hips mimicked what she'd done to him. She went up on tiptoe while her hands found the hem of his shirt and pulled it out of his trousers. The second her fingers connected with his bare flesh all sane thoughts flew out of her mind.

"God, Izzy." He wrenched his mouth away again. "You're so hard to resist."

"Then don't stop," she said as she trailed her hands from his back to his belly, connecting with a solid mass of muscle.

Now that she'd made the decision to move forward with the relationship, she wanted to experience everything with him.

His hand closed over hers, halting her upward movement. "As much as I really want to continue with this, I promised Zeke we'd go, and I don't break my promises."

"Fine," she said pouting dramatically.

He laughed and kissed the tip of her nose. "Trust me when I say, this isn't over." His voice dropped a few octaves on the last three words and she shivered in response.

"I can't wait."

"Well, you're going to have to wait a little longer. Have you got everything?" he asked as he tucked his shirt back in.

"Yep, let me just go grab my purse and make sure the back patio doors are locked."

"I have a better idea."

"What's that?" she asked.

"You get your purse and I'll check that your doors are locked."

Isabella cocked her head to look at him. Did he think she

couldn't be trusted to lock her own doors? "You know I've been living by myself for years and am quite capable of locking my own doors."

He huffed out a sigh. "I know, but this is part of me and who I am."

She stared silently at him, his words reminding her of their first meeting.

No way was she going to let him get away with thinking that because they were embarking on a relationship together, he could become controlling with her. "Want to tell me what this is all about?" she asked, placing her hands on her hips and tapping her foot like she did when she was waiting for one of her students to explain how a pot of paint was splattered on the floor.

"What? What am I doing?"

Isabella rolled her eyes but quit tapping her foot and re-laxed her arms to the side. "What's with the whole 'me GI Joe, you damsel in distress'? Because, let me tell you, I'm far from being helpless."

With two steps he'd closed the distance between them and placed his hands softly on her shoulders. "I'm sorry, Izzy. I can't help doing what I just did. I do it to my mom and it drives her batty too, especially since Dad doesn't act this way. Sometimes, I just can't switch off my training. I told you I'm the first into a building after the initial breach. Sam's and my job is to make sure there are no surprises for the team."

"Okay, I can understand that, but this is my house, Ethan. I was inside it and in the kitchen before you arrived at my door. I know there's nothing lurking there that's a threat. Plus, I know I locked the door but before I go out I *always* give it one last check."

A frustrated breath blew out of him and he ran his fingers over his closely cropped hair. Had he had a haircut since she'd last seen him? Shaking off her random thought she waited to see what he was going to say next. "Fine. I'll wait here while you check the doors."

There was a fine line they were treading here, one they needed to work out how to traverse before either one of them fell off—again.

After looking at for a few more seconds, she sighed and walked around him and into the kitchen where she'd left her purse. Striding over to the doors, Isabella tugged the handle down, confirming they were locked.

She took a few seconds to stare out over her backyard and center herself. Who knew relationships could be so fraught with clashes? Travis's and her relationship had been smooth sailing. Would it have lasted the distance? She'd never asked herself that question before. Hadn't seen any need. With the confidence of a teenager, she'd been sure they'd whether any storm. Now she had to wonder if they wouldn't have fallen apart at the first sign of trouble.

But Travis and their past wasn't what she should be worrying about. Ethan was her here and now, and that was where her focus needed to be.

Isabella jumped when warm hands landed on her shoulders and turned her to face Ethan. "Are you okay?" he whispered as he cupped her cheek.

Words lodged in her throat so she nodded and slipped her arms around his waist and hugged him. "Yeah, I'm sorry for not understanding this part of you."

He pressed a soft kiss on her hair. "It's all part of getting to know one another. You can't say our path to each other is going to be boring. And I'm excited to get to know you, Izzy. Very excited."

"Me too." And she was, there was no denying it, she liked Ethan—an awful lot.

ETHAN SIDE-EYED ISABELLA as he turned the car off. Through the whole drive to Zeke's place she'd been quiet, answering questions when he asked but otherwise, content to sit and watch the scenery pass by. The silence hadn't been awkward, like he'd expected it to be. It had been the opposite, in fact, he hadn't minded it.

"You ready?" he asked as he unclipped his seat belt.

She followed his action and picked up her purse from where she'd placed it on the floor when she'd gotten into the car. "As ready as I'll ever be."

Needing to erase the scared look on her face he leaned

across the console, hooking a finger under her chin and turning her so she faced him. "They're going to love you, Isabella Knowles. Trust me on that, how could they not?"

"Oh, plenty of reasons why they won't like me. You guys are a team and I'm sure the women in the relationships will all be watching me closely to make sure I'm worthy of being with one of their own."

Ethan chuckled. As much as he wanted to deny it, what Isabella said was pretty much the truth. Zeke's wife, Anna, had sent him a dozen texts when she found out he was bringing a date to the party. He'd answered her questions, but also warned the other woman that if she so much as made Isabella uncomfortable they'd be out of there. That had earned him a few choice words and deadly looks from Zeke. His brother-in-arms protected his woman as much as Ethan was going to protect Isabella.

A stab of guilt pierced his gut. He hadn't mentioned his possible promotion to anyone. He was still mulling everything over, the promotion and his reenlistment. Prior to meeting Isabella, it would've been a no-brainer. Reenlist and accept the promotion.

A week ago, he was still on track with that train of thought. Now, after finding out what Isabella had been through with her short marriage and committing to moving forward with their relationship, it wasn't a straightforward decision. He never thought he'd give up his career for someone. He admired his mother for what she'd done, but she was ready. He wasn't. He didn't know if he'd ever be. And there were no guarantees that his relationship with Isabella would even go the long distance.

He had hopes it would. But giving up everything he'd worked hard for over a woman wasn't a decision he could make lightly. He liked to think they could reach a compromise. Ethan recalled Isabella saying her dream had been to be a military wife. Maybe deep down that dream was still within her.

"Ethan? You okay?" Isabella squeezed his hand, pulling him back to the here and now.

"I am, and so will you, Izzy. It's going to be a good afternoon, and if I have to, I'll go all GI Joe on them." He finished with a wink.

The comment had the desired effect and she laughed, a little of the deer-in-headlights look disappearing from her face. "I may just have to see that happen."

Ethan closed the gap and placed his lips softly over hers. She melted against him and it took all his self-control not to thread his fingers through her hair and devour her. Walking into the party with messed-up hair and lipstick smeared everywhere was a look he was sure she didn't want to present to his friends.

He pulled his lips away. "Come on, let's go."

He got out of the car and dashed around to her side so that he could open the door for her. Closing the door, he grabbed her hand, linked their fingers together, and walked down the driveway.

Zeke had told him to head straight for the backyard. The muted sound of conversations got louder the farther down the pavement they went. Isabella's fingers squeezed his and he'd have to be on another planet not to work out that the nerves she talked about earlier were back. He'd feel the same if he were about to walk into a room filled with her work colleagues.

They rounded the corner and the second they walked through the gate all eyes turned to them.

Great, this was the last thing he wanted. He'd been hoping to ease Isabella into meeting everyone.

Anna broke through the small crowd, a big smile on her face and her hand cupped under her pregnant belly. "Ethan. So glad you could make it." She breezed up to him and kissed him on the cheek.

"Hey, Anna, glad to be here. This is Isabella Knowles. Isabella, this is Anna Hopkins, the hostess and Zeke's wife."

Out of the corner of his eye, he caught the movement of Isabella pulling herself up a little straighter and holding out her hand. "Hi, Anna, it's nice to meet you. Thanks for having me."

"It's great to meet you, Isabella. And no hand shaking here, I'm a hugger." Anna smiled big and grabbed Isabella. "Come meet everyone," she said. As they walked away, Anna looked over her shoulder and winked at him. "You know where the drinks are don't you, Ethan?"

Ethan didn't know whether he wanted to shake or hug Anna and her antics. "Yeah, I do. And, Anna?"

The woman raised her eyebrow. "Yes?"

"Be nice."

"Always," she said on a laugh.

For a few heartbeats, he watched as Anna introduced Isabella around. At the first sign of distress from his girl, he'd be in there, breaking her free. But she seemed relaxed and smiled at everyone she met. Ethan walked over to the row of coolers set against the wall under the back porch. He had to lift a couple of lids before he found the one containing sodas and pulled a can out of the ice.

The sound of giggles had him glancing over his shoulder and he spied Isabella surrounded by women and they were looking at him. Ethan resisted the urge to check to see if he'd split his pants. But, surely, if the seams of his jeans had ripped apart he would've heard it. Instead he raised his can in a silent salute and popped the tab, all the while hoping his red boxer briefs weren't on display for the whole party to see.

"Am I a master matchmaker or what?"

Dragging his gaze away from his girl, Ethan spun around to face who'd spoken to him. Seeing the smug look on Lincoln's face, he was tempted to wipe it off. He couldn't deny, Linc had knocked this one out of the park. But no way was he going to let his friend know that. "I wouldn't say a master, because prior to Izzy, your setups had been pretty abysmal."

"Izzy, huh? You guys *that* friendly."

Ethan gritted his teeth to keep from snapping at Linc's sleazy comment. "Watch it." He took another sip of his drink.

All the amusement dancing in Lincoln's eyes disappeared, to be replaced by a thoughtful look.

Shit.

Had he given his growing feelings for Isabella away to his friend? What he should've done was brush off Linc's comment as an inconsequential remark. Fortunately, Zeke wandered up to them, oblivious to the tension simmering between both of them.

"Well, looks like your girl has got the Anna seal of approval," Zeke commented and tapped his beer bottle against the soda can in Ethan's hand.

"Looks that way," he murmured as the women chatted and welcomed Isabella into the fold. When he invited her to this party, his hope was to not remind her of her loss but to show her the unity she'd seen from those women who took her in when her mom deserted her was still here. Anna was certainly going out of her way to help him with that message.

"She's definitely hot, maybe I should've said I'd go on a blind date with her instead of setting the two of you up," Linc commented. Normally Ethan could deal with Linc's teasing and innuendo, but today it grated on him worse than fingernails down a chalkboard did.

"Shut up, Linc. You'd never had lasted the first date."

Lincoln laughed. "Oh, you have it so bad."

Ethan took a step toward him, clenching his fist at his side. He'd never wanted to hit his friend before, but if he made one more smart-ass comment about Isabella, Linc was going to become intimately acquainted with his left hook.

Zeke stepped between the both of them. "Knock it off, you two. I've got a wife who is a couple weeks away from giving birth to our first child, I don't want any fights here. Do you understand? It's a party, so lighten up and enjoy yourselves."

Ethan unclenched his fist and took a couple of deep breaths. The last thing he wanted to do was create a scene. A quick look around the yard showed that no one was paying attention to him and Linc. The only person watching him was Isabella. She was now seated with the other girls. Her eyebrow rose in question and she mouthed the words, *"Are you okay?"* Even from this distance, he could make out the worry in her eyes.

Consciously, relaxing his facial muscles, he smiled and winked while he nodded and mouth back *yes* to her.

A frown marred her forehead and she looked like she was about to get up from her chair when the person beside her placed a hand on her arm and directed her attention away from him. Relief swept through him and he looked over to his friend.

"Sorry, Linc, but yeah, I'm glad you set us up."

Chapter Eleven

"ARE YOU SURE I can't tempt you with some dessert?"

"No thanks. If I eat another mouthful I'm going to burst." Isabella looked at their hostess and smiled.

She liked the other woman. Anna had done everything possible to make her feel welcome and part of the group. There was only one girl, Amy, who didn't seem to make an effort to interact with everyone. She spent most of the time on her phone. Amy was here with a guy named Caleb, who Isabella also found out was Ethan's roommate when he introduced them.

During their talks, Ethan had mentioned a roommate but he never named him. All the girls were worried about Caleb. From the second she'd been introduced to Ethan's roommate she'd seen the hollow look in his eyes, like every breath hurt and he was there in body but not in spirit. There was a story there, one she wanted to ask Ethan about but didn't feel it was her place to.

Isabella looked around the kitchen and saw the mass of dishes piled everywhere. "Are you sure I can't help you with this?" she asked again.

Anna laughed. "Nope, follow me and watch and learn."

As Anna waddled toward the back door, Isabella shook her head in amazement. Why a woman who was only a couple weeks away from having her first baby was having a party was beyond her, but Anna had waved off her concerns like she'd waved off Isabella's outstretched hand when they'd first me.

When Anna opened the back door, Isabella stood to the side, so she could *watch and learn.*

"Okay, boys, clean-up time."

All the men standing in the backyard put their drinks down and filed into the kitchen. When Ethan passed he dropped a kiss on her nose.

"That's very impressive," she commented once the last man walked past her.

Anna grabbed Isabella's arm and hooked it through her own. Together they walked outside to join the group of women sitting around the unlit firepit. "That, my dear Isabella, is the only reason I agreed to having this party. Zeke promised me he and the boys would do everything from grill the meat to clean up afterward. All I had to do was organize for the girls to bring salads and desserts. It's the perfect way to have a barbeque, if you ask me."

Now that she really examined the last few hours, the guys here had done all the hard work. They'd done it so seamlessly she hadn't noticed it until it had been pointed out to her.

"So, Isabella, Patricia tells me you're a schoolteacher.

You're a braver woman than me," Amy said out of the blue.

"Some days are better than others."

"I don't think I could ever do it," Amy continued. "I like my life the way it is."

Isabella might regret asking the question, but she wanted to get to know everyone, even if the vibe Amy was giving off was one of superiority. "What is that you do?"

"I'm not working. My daddy set me up with a trust fund so I can do whatever I want, whenever I want."

Now that would be nice, to not work and still buy whatever one wanted. But Isabella suspected she'd get bored very quickly if that were her life. It also began to make sense why Caleb was seeing Amy—she was a no-commitment type of girl. Isabella didn't know Caleb's story, but the stand-down vibes he had given off all day suggested he wasn't into long-term.

Ultimately, they're relationship wasn't any of her business, and Amy might not be around at the next get-together anyhow.

Wait. What? Next get-together?

Isabella was getting ahead of herself, but she couldn't deny that being back among a group of military wives and girlfriends reminded her of the times other mothers had welcomed her into their homes. And of the short time she'd lived on base with Travis.

Looking around at the women gathered near her, Isabella began to feel a semblance of confidence build inside of her that if she and Ethan did deepen their relationship that when he went away she wouldn't be alone.

Of course, she also had Meredith, but her best friend wouldn't understand the loneliness and worry that went along with being a military partner like these women would.

"Your kitchen is now sparkling clean." Ethan's voice near Isabella's ear startled her out of her introspection. His hair was slightly mussed, his shirt sporting the odd spot of water—he looked delicious and she wanted to lose herself in him.

Without thinking about their audience, she closed the small gap between them and wound her arms around his neck. Automatically his arms looped her waist. Isabella went up on tiptoe and kissed him. If he was surprised by her assertiveness he didn't let on, he just pulled her tighter and deepened the kiss.

Eventually the sound of whistles, clapping, and calls *to get a room* penetrated the sensual fog that had enveloped her and Ethan. She ducked her head against his chest.

What on earth had she been thinking?

"Well," Ethan said, clearing his throat. "I think that's our cue to leave."

Laughter sounded around the group and a wave of heat filled her cheeks.

Summoning some sort of control when she literally had none, Isabella extracted herself from his hold and walked back to Anna. "Thanks for making me feel so welcome," she said, hoping against hope the other woman wouldn't make a comment about what she and Ethan had just done.

Anna pulled her close for another hug. "It's no hardship. The smile you bring to Ethan's face makes me happy. Hope to see you soon."

"I'd like that," Isabella said. "Maybe I can grab your number from Ethan?"

"Definitely and once you text me I'll add you to our group chat." Anna smiled up to Zeke who'd wrapped his arm around his wife while Isabella had been talking to her.

"That would be great, thanks."

If she thought she was going to get out of the party with just a quick hug to Anna, she was mistaken. The rest of the girls all lined up to give her a hug while the boys all teased Ethan.

Finally, they were able to head to their car. "Well, I don't have to ask if you had a good time tonight," he commented as he slung an arm around her shoulder, holding her close to him.

"I did. I'd forgotten this."

"Forgotten what?"

"That the military partners are as tight-knit as the soldiers themselves." While she'd had a good time and had felt welcomed by everyone, it put extra pressure on her. What if she and Ethan didn't work out? What would they think of her then?

Conversation stopped as he unlocked the car and held

the door open for her. And that was okay. Ethan naturally held doors open for women, not to be condescending but because his mom had taught him to treat a woman like a lady.

She was all for independence; she'd been living it for the last few years. But this was the first time the person she was dating went out of their way to do little things that made her feel special.

Once they were on the road, Ethan started the conversation up again. "Anna pulled me aside and said she really liked you. She's a tough nut to crack, but I think she liked you on sight."

"She was very welcoming, and I can't believe she's so close to having a baby but still had a party."

Ethan chuckled. "Oh, there was no way she wasn't going to have this party. Anna loves to entertain and even if her due date was tomorrow she'd still have had it. Plus, Zeke did promise we'd do all the work." He paused as he signaled to join the traffic on the highway. "I'm glad you enjoyed yourself. I know it can't have been easy after all this time."

Again, she squeezed his leg, she really could get used to touching him. "It was a really relaxing party. The girls are really nice and not…"

God, how did she say what she wanted to say without offending him? The last thing she wanted to do was offend Ethan and he'd leave the second he dropped her off.

"They're not what?"

Blowing out a breath she transferred her gaze out the window, so she wouldn't have to see his face when she spoke. "They weren't what I expected. They were nice and open and welcoming. I'd forgotten what it was like. I guess in my mind I'd romanticized the memories of my childhood, to make it better than thinking I was the reason my mom always bailed the second Dad was deployed. That she couldn't stand being around me and that the only reason everyone was nice was because they felt sorry for me."

"I don't believe that for a second. I've lived on bases when my dad was transferred. Everyone was always friendly. Sure, there was the odd person who kept to themselves. And by no means do I think living on or near a base is a walk in the park. It can be a hard life but rewarding. No way do I think the families who looked after you felt sorry for you. They did it because they cared."

Once again, she tried to pull her hand away but, this time, Ethan closed his fingers tighter around hers and lifted her hand to his mouth, brushing his lips softly across the top. "Plus, I know you offered to help Anna a couple of times. That always goes down well with everyone. It shows that you think as part of a team, which is really important when involved with someone in the service."

Isabella let Ethan's words sink in. He'd been right when he'd said she'd offered to help. How could she not? She was a guest in someone's house, it would be rude not to offer some sort of assistance. "I guess. I always wondered why

Mom never tried to get along with the other women. I mean, she knew the chances of moving around on a regular basis was a given when she married Dad. I've never asked Dad about the early stages of his and Mom's relationship. He seemed happier when she left us."

"I don't know, maybe that's something you need to ask him. Perhaps you need to discuss your past issues in order to move forward and build a new and better one together."

Isabella liked to think her relationship with Dad was changing for the better in a permanent way. Their earlier phone call had already splintered the ice that encased their relationship, now it was time to shatter the frozen block and move forward in their father/daughter partnership.

"Yeah, I think you're right. He was happy when he heard I was still seeing you. I think it's one of the reasons he wants to meet you."

"Really? Why is that?" Ethan relinquished the hold he had on her hand so he could place both hands on the wheel as he turned down her street.

"I believe he wants to see the fruits of his matchmaking skills."

"Oh, God, no wonder he and Linc get on so well. Linc was unbearable today."

Isabella laughed as she remembered the cheeky smile he'd given her when Ethan had introduced them. She had expected him to corner her and ask her endless questions about what she and Ethan were up to. The fact he hadn't had her wondering if it was because of the man sitting beside her. "He appears to be a fun guy when I met him today."

"Oh, yeah, he's an unhealthy growth for sure," Ethan muttered when he pulled into her driveway.

She burst out laughing. "Oh, my God, Ethan, that was terrible."

"Terrible but true. And, in answer to your question, yes, I told him to stay away from you. I didn't want him to tell you all about my bad habits." He finished with a wink.

Unconsciously, her tongue dipped out and swiped over her lips. An invisible line connected the two of them and by some magical force, she found herself leaning forward at the same time as Ethan. Their lips collided and she sighed at the feathery touch. Her eyes drifted shut and she raised her hands and rested them on his chest. Beneath the soft fabric of his shirt, his heart beat frantically against her fingers.

A groan echoed around the car and Ethan pulled his lips away from hers. The light from the streetlamp by her house filled the car with a golden glow, highlighting the sleek plane of his nose, his angular cheekbones. But what made her catch her breath the most, was the desire burning brightly in his eyes.

"Do you want to come in?" she whispered, not wanting to speak too loudly to break the spell surrounding them. The silence stretched and Isabella couldn't help but wonder if he was having a debate with himself as to whether accepting her invitation was a wise one or not.

None of his hesitation made sense though. He'd seemed with her every step of the way during their very public kiss at the barbeque, like he hadn't wanted it to end. She was giving him the green light here, why wasn't he putting his foot down and driving through?

Now would be a good time for the world to stop so she wouldn't have to live through a rejection. Dating sucked sometimes.

Ethan smiled. "Yes."

Without thinking she punched him lightly on the arm.

"Hey," he said rubbing the spot. "What was that for?"

"That was for taking so long to answer my question and making me think I'd made a complete utter fool of myself." And way to go on making a fool of herself by being brutally honest with him.

"I'm sorry, Izzy, I didn't want to make you feel this way. I just…"

Now it was his turn to hesitate. They were quite the pair. "You were just what?"

He ran a hand through his hair, then sighed and grabbed her hand, running his thumb across the top of it. A shiver wracked her body at the light touch.

"Izzy, I've been attracted to you from the second I spied you wearing that red fedora. Even when you walked out the door, I wished for fate to somehow intervene so that we would meet up again. And it did. We've had so many false starts that, as much as I want to go inside with you, I want to know that you are totally on board with this."

Every single word he said penetrated the hard shell she'd put up to protect her heart, the one that was already beginning to disperse with every passing second in his company. With Ethan, all her defenses were being attacked, and instead of being afraid and scared, she was beginning to feel empowered.

"I'm totally on board, Ethan. I want you to come inside. I want to spend the night with you."

Reaching for the door handle, she opened the door and got out. Before shutting the door, she leaned down and gazed inside the car. "Are you coming or not?"

By the way Ethan scrambled out of the car, the double meaning wasn't lost on him. He was by her side in a flash. "You, Ms. Knowles, are extremely tempting."

"Well, that's good, Mr. Masters," she said as she pushed her key into the lock. "Because you are very tempting too."

The second they were inside with the door shut, Ethan's arms were around her and his lips crashed down on hers. In her sensual haze, she registered the sound of her purse and keys crashing to the ground. Her arms wound around his neck and she went up on her tiptoes to deepen the kiss.

A groan sounded against her mouth and Ethan pulled back. "Where's your bedroom?"

Taking a step away from him, she laced her fingers through his and silently led him down the hallway. With every step, her heart beat harder and faster, anticipation sizzling through her. The last time she'd been with a guy had been less than memorable. She wasn't going to have the same problem with Ethan. Just his kisses set her aflame.

In her room, she let go of his hand and headed over to her nightstand. A second later, the room glowed with the ambient light of her bedside lamp, and all her bravado disappeared when she turned to see Ethan standing in her room. She licked her lips.

God, seriously, why was she acting like she'd never done this before? Because she hadn't. Oh, she'd had sex since she'd been widowed, but she'd never made the conscious decision to seduce a man. A man who was beginning to mean more to her than any other man had.

Would he make the first move? As if he could read her mind, Ethan began a slow stalk toward her, his fingers going to the buttons of his shirt. By the time he stopped in front of her, his shirt was undone, and she caught a glimpse of tanned flesh. Even the small expanse of skin she could see made her want to rip the shirt off and run her hands all over him.

Only she didn't want to rush this moment. The need to make this evening special splintered through her.

"Do you have any idea how gorgeous you look?" he whispered, as he answered her unspoken wish and pulled his shirt off his shoulders.

"Do you have any idea how handsome you are?" she countered and closed the small gap between them. She couldn't deny the overpowering desire to touch him any longer. Resting her hands against his hard chest, she rose up on tiptoe and nipped at his lips. She withdrew, but an arm clamped around her waist and held her flush against him.

Warmth pooled between her legs and his mouth took full possession of hers as he ran his tongue along the seam of her slightly parted lips, encouraging her to open farther for him. The second she did, his tongue invaded her mouth, dueling with hers.

Her body pulsed beneath the onslaught. Waves of desire built inside of her, consuming her. But it wasn't enough. She wanted no restrictions between them. Keeping her lips fused to his, she lowered her hands to his jeans, finding the end of the belt and threading it through the buckle to release the strip of leather. She popped the button and found the metal tab of his zipper. Before she could even pull it down a millimeter, his hand closed over hers.

What?

Did he want to stop?

Had he changed his mind?

"There's no rush, Izzy. We've got all night. I'm not going anywhere," he murmured against her neck as he nibbled at her skin. The action sent shivers coursing through her bloodstream.

Perhaps he was right. Perhaps there was no rush to reach the finish line. How many times had she rushed through things only to be disappointed at the end result? Too many times with the few guys she'd slept with. The last guy would be snoozing beside her on the bed by now while she'd still be waiting for the main event to happen. Ethan wouldn't keep her waiting. He'd ensure she was the main event before he joined her at the finish line.

His lips began a slow, seductive trail along her jawline to her earlobe, where he sucked the small piece of flesh into his mouth. His teeth tugging lightly on the gold hoop she wore.

While his mouth was busy teasing her ears, his hands were roaming all over her back, bunching her sundress around her hips. God, how she wanted his hands on her bare flesh. No, not only his hands, but his wicked tongue and mouth. She wanted him to kiss her all over. Just thinking about it encouraged another rush of moisture between her thighs.

"Undress me, Ethan. Please undress me." She whimpered when his hands dipped beneath the light fabric of her dress and cupped her ass. Unable to help herself, she ground her hips against his erection and was rewarded with a moan from Ethan.

Screw taking it slow. Her fingers fumbled until she found his zipper and pulled it down as he found the hidden zipper of her dress and gently tugged. Cool breeze from the air conditioner hit the exposed skin and she shivered.

One second she was standing by her bed, her hand grabbing his jeans to thrust them down, the next she was flat on her bed wearing just her panties and Ethan had settled himself between her legs, his long, hard erection jutting from his belly. Her fingers itched to wrap around and stroke him, feel the hard steel encased in satiny soft skin.

"You are so beautiful, Isabella. You have no idea what seeing you like this is doing to me."

His dick bobbed and she couldn't stop the smile from breaking out even if she wanted to. "I have a good idea."

"Wench, you'll pay for that." He trailed his fingers over her belly.

"I'm gonna hold you to that." She lifted her hips a fraction to let Ethan know exactly what she wanted from him.

He lowered his head and her body tightened in anticipation of the moment when his lips would enclose over her silky folds. Her eyes drifted shut as she willed herself to relax.

His lips and tongue kissed and laved her inner thigh, his fingers feathering down her other thigh. Just when she thought he was going to finally give her what she wanted, he totally bypassed her core and placed soft kisses on her belly. His hands smoothed up her sides, stopping at her breasts. Her nipples puckered in the cool air, and she moaned when his lips closed over one of the distended peaks. Again her hips lifted and collided with his dick; she ground against him, creating a delicious friction that combined with his mouth on her breast.

How she wanted him filling her until they were joined so tightly they couldn't tell where each of them started.

"I need you inside of me, Ethan. I can't wait any longer."

"Soon, Izzy, soon," he said against her skin.

Her moan of displeasure soon turned to a groan of delight as he sucked her silken folds into his mouth. Her head thrashed against the pillow as his tongue laved, licked, and bit her sensitive bundle of nerves. Her orgasm built in her toes and traversed up her legs. Isabella gripped the bedsheets and cried out loud with the release, her body shaking with the force of her climax. Ethan kept licking her, prolonging her orgasm until she crashed over the edge again.

Her erratic breathing echoed around the room as her heart thumped loudly in her chest.

"You okay, Izzy?" Ethan asked as she heard a crinkle. Another shudder ripped through her at the sound.

"I will be the second you get inside of me."

He chuckled and the next instant he was laying over her, his dick nudging at her entrance. "Your wish is my command."

He slid into her easily. Their mingled sighs of pleasure competed with the low hum of the air conditioner. Fully seated in her, Ethan paused—was he giving her time to adjust or did he need a moment to compose himself? It didn't matter. She reveled in the sensation.

After a few seconds, he raised himself and retreated from her body before thrusting back in. He repeated the motion in a slow, measured movement, drawing out her pleasure. As his pace increased, so did their sounds of pleasure.

Isabella hooked her legs around his waist, angling her

hips to send his thrusts deeper. The new angle ensured he hit her G-spot, and she bit down on his shoulder to stop from screaming out. But nothing could stop her from voicing the desire strumming through her.

"Oh, God, Ethan, I can't take much more."

His ragged breathing was loud in her ear. "Neither can I," he said, and his rhythm faltered for a moment before becoming faster, smoother.

This time her orgasm started at the base of her spine, tingling through her nerve endings until they all met at her core and she exploded all around him. Her inner muscles clenched tightly around Ethan, and she knew the moment his release hit him. Not because of the way he shouted her name, but because of the way he jerked inside of her, totally out of control. It was wonderful.

Ethan gathered her close and rolled them so she was lying on top of him, their bodies still spasming as they came down from their high.

Isabella closed her eyes and snuggled closer. Nothing in her life was better than this moment.

Chapter Twelve

ETHAN GLANCED FROM the road to Isabella in the passenger seat. Her hands were resting on her thighs and her fingers were tapping out a rapid beat. The closer they got to her dad's house, the more tense she became. If anyone should be nervous it should be him. After all, he was meeting her father for the first time.

He laid his hand over one of hers, stilling her nervous movements. "It's going to be fine, Izzy. I have your six."

Her fingers gripped his and he controlled the shaft of desire flowing through him. Last night had been amazing and waking up in her arms had been even better. If he hadn't heard the tail end of her conversation with her dad the previous evening, he would've persuaded her to stay in bed with him all day. But he had and going to see her father today was a big step in their relationship. No way did he want to come between father and daughter.

"It's not like we're going into a battle or anything. It's lunch with my dad."

"Aren't we? I realize we haven't known each other very long, but from our conversations, you've alluded to a strained relationship between you and your dad."

"I don't know what our relationship is at the moment. It goes from good to bad. I want it to stay good." Isabella sighed.

He wanted to pull her in his arms and hold her close. Not possible considering he was driving, but the second they arrived at her father's house, that was what he planned to do.

"Why don't you tell me a little about him? You said he was in the army and then joined a special forces team."

The most elite team in the army was Delta Force. If Isabella's father was part of that he'd have kept his job pretty quiet from her. The less she knew the safer she'd be.

"Yeah, he never talked much about what he did. There were times I'd come home from school and find June at the house. I was thirteen when my mom left, and seeing as I pretty much had looked after myself from the age of six, the fact he wasn't there didn't bother me too much."

"Who's June?"

"I suppose you could say she was my nanny. She would stay with me until Dad returned. She was wonderful, but because I was still confused about Mom leaving, I was more of a brat than I should've been."

Ethan squeezed her hand again. "I'm sure she understood. Maybe you should look her up. Does your dad still know where she lives?"

"I can't."

Her response was immediate and curt. Okay, best to

leave that matter lie. "Does your dad do any sort of work now?"

"Yeah, he works at one of the big box hardware stores. He loves to help people with their DIY projects. If he could, I'm sure he'd go over there and do it with them."

Ethan chuckled. "I think I'm going to like your dad. I don't mind the odd DIY project."

"Great, just what I need, two guys who think they can fix anything." Isabella groaned and it took him back to the previous evening when she groaned as she climaxed around him. He shifted in his seat in an attempt to alleviate his growing hard-on.

"I promise not to encourage your dad to talk about his favorite brand of power tool."

He was pleased she smiled. It didn't quite reach her eyes, but at least it was better than the frown that had been marring her forehead the whole drive.

"I'm going to hold you to that one, Ethan Masters."

"Anytime. I keep my promises."

Well, he tried really hard and so far he'd been able to keep his word with his dealings with Isabella. His GPS broke the silence that had descended around them and he followed the instruction to turn right; in five hundred feet his destination would be on the left.

When they pulled into the driveway, he turned the engine off and studied the bungalow in front of him. The walls appeared to be freshly painted and in the corner of the front porch sat a swinging love seat. Everything about the place looked meticulously looked after and showed the person who lived inside took pride in their home.

He glanced over at Isabella and studied her as she kept staring at the house. "How long has it been since you've been here?" he asked.

"A while," she responded quietly. He waited for her to make the move to get out of the car. The second her spine straightened and she pushed her shoulders back he knew she'd made her decision. "Let's go."

Not giving her a chance to back out, he released his seat belt at the same time as she did hers. Her hand reached out for the door handle and he reached over and squeezed her thigh. "Let me."

She nodded and leaned down to pick her purse up off the floor in front of her. Her fingers gripped the leather, another sign that nerves still resided inside of her.

When he opened her door he held out his hand, relieved when she placed hers in it without any argument. He liked knowing she was leaning on him for support.

They'd taken two steps when she stopped.

"What's wrong?"

"I didn't bring anything. How could I not bring anything?"

Tugging her so she fell against him, he slipped his free arm around her and lowered his head until she had no option but to look up at him. "I don't think your dad will expect you to bring anything. He'll be glad to see you, and remember, you're not in this alone. I'm right here beside you."

He didn't give her a chance to respond, just closed the small gap between them and kissed her gently. The kiss wasn't like the carnal ones they'd shared the previous evening. This was a kiss to reiterate everything he'd just said to her. Her body softened against his and he willed his growing erection to subside. What a great first impression that would make, walking into his girlfriend's father's house with the telltale bulge outlining his jeans.

Reluctantly, he severed their connection and rested his forehead against hers. Her breath puffing out against his chin. Nothing was better than standing like this with her.

"Can we stay like this forever?" she asked on a sigh.

"Would be nice but I'd prefer to be in a house than in your dad's driveway."

A little laugh rippled through her and the tension inside of her appeared to have dissipated between his kiss and their embrace. "Yeah, not sure Dad will be too impressed." Putting a little distance between them she reached up and swiped her finger across his lips, his body jerked at the touch and he resisted the urge to chase her finger and suck it into his mouth. "That shade doesn't suit you."

Geez, he needed to get his mind out of the gutter and into meeting-the-father mode. This flirting needed to stop, but hell, it was so much fun. "Shame, I thought it would be nice to match when we met your dad."

"Are you two planning to stay out there for the whole of your visit?" A gruff voice broke through their little cocoon and he automatically stood straighter.

Turning, he saw a tall man standing on the porch. Like Ethan, he wore his hair in a short buzz cut and had on jeans and a button-down shirt. Well, if two people were going to match, it was he and Isabella's dad.

"Showtime," Isabella muttered beside him. "Hi, Dad, it's good to see you."

Isabella made no attempt to move toward the house and he wasn't going to force her to move until she was good and ready to.

As if sensing his daughter's reluctance, her dad stepped off the porch and approached the two of them. The second he got close enough to them, the other man's face split into a wide grin and in two strides he swept Isabella up into a warm hug. "Honey bee, you're a sight for sore eyes."

Honey bee?

Ethan didn't know what surprised him the most, her dad's nickname for her or her wide-eyed look at being hugged by her dad. Did they not normally hug when they saw each other? His mom always greeted him with a warm embrace and a sloppy kiss on the cheek. His dad, the obligatory slap-on-the-back-man-hug. He imagined when he took Isabella to meet his folks they'd do the same to her, although Dad wouldn't slap her on the back. After seeing Isabella's reaction to her father's hug, he might have to warn them not to get so friendly.

And he totally needed to slow down. What he needed to concentrate on was getting through this day and then he could look at what was going to happen tomorrow. It wasn't like his life was clear-cut at the moment. He had decisions to make, and he'd been putting them off. Soon he wouldn't be able to ignore them.

"Dad, this is Ethan Masters. Ethan, my dad, Eric Knowles."

Ethan stepped forward and held out his hand. "Sir, it's nice to meet you." Eric grasped his hand in a firm hold. He would expect nothing less of her father and an ex-military man.

"Good to meet you too. How about we continue this conversation inside where it's cool?"

When he turned, Ethan couldn't help but notice the precision of his turn. He had no idea how long Eric had been out of the military, but he certainly hadn't lost the skills that had been drummed into him.

Ethan waited until Isabella's dad was a couple of steps ahead of them before he slipped his arm back around her waist. "You okay?" he murmured in her ear.

Holding her so close to him, it was impossible to miss the full body shiver that ripped through her when his lips connected with her ear. His body answered with one of its own.

"Yeah, it was just the…"

"The hug?" he finished for her.

"Yep, he's not usually big on affection."

The uncertainty in her voice almost killed him and he wished there was a way he could rip it out of her. No one should ever question signs of affection from their parents.

"Just remember, I'm here for you. Any time you want to leave, let me know."

"Thank you," she said softly and kissed him on the cheek. "I do feel like I can face anything with you by my side."

Her words filled him with hope, that a future was possible for them. The more time he spent with her the more he wanted to always come home to her. "That's what I'm here for, Izzy."

"Well, I hope that's not all," she said on a laugh as they entered the house.

"I promise I'll show you later exactly what else I'm here for." Again her body reacted with a delicious little shimmer and he made himself think of repetitive marching drills in an attempt to control his ever rising erection.

SO FAR, SO good.

The words whispered through Isabella's mind as the front door clicked shut behind Ethan. He'd offered to get more beer, at her father's suggestion of course. They'd gotten through lunch without too many landmines exploding. She didn't have to be a rocket scientist to know her father wanted to spend some alone time with her to quiz her about Ethan.

"I like him, honey bee. And it's clear he likes you. How about you? What do you think of your young man?"

All day, Dad had been calling her honey bee. When Ethan had called her Izzy she'd let herself believe he was the first man to give her a nickname. Travis had always called her Isabella. But she was wrong. Like the memories of June, she'd pushed her father's nickname to the far recesses of her mind. She'd believed she'd been doing it for her own good, dwelling on the past was never a good thing, especially if that past wasn't pleasant. But slowly and surely, good times were beginning to filter back into her consciousness, reminding her that not everything had been bad and the rift between her and her father was of her doing, not his. She'd pushed him away because she thought it would keep her safe.

"Isabella? Are you okay?"

While she'd been strolling through her memories, her dad had moved off his chair and was squatting in front of her, his hand hovering above her knee.

"Yeah, Dad, I'm good. Better than I've been in a while and, in answer to your question, I like Ethan too."

The smile splitting her dad's face told her all she needed to know. But she needed to stop him from getting any ideas.

"Stop whatever it is you're thinking, Dad."

He moved back to his chair. "What am I thinking?" he said, attempting to widen his eyes in innocence.

Had he always been this fun?

Yes, he'd always teased and joked with her, but after Mom left them, Isabella had put up a barrier and things went from good to bad. She had blamed him for Mom walking out, even though life had been better once she'd been gone. She'd maintained that wall even though she thought she'd been letting him in. How wrong she'd been.

"You're thinking dresses and churches and flowers."

He shrugged and lifted his bottle of light beer to his lips. "A dad's job is to make sure his daughter is well looked after and with the right man. And you're happier than I've seen you in a long time."

"Oh, for goodness' sake, Dad, we've only just started dating. Anything could happen. He could be hiding terrible habits and hasn't shown them to me yet."

Her dad burst out laughing. "Who are you trying to convince?" He leaned forward and waited for her to do the same, which she did. She waited for an invisible cone to close down on them, like their conversation had to be conducted without prying ears. "Honey bee, I know things between us haven't been easy. I know I should've tried harder to bridge the gap, but I'm a man, a military man at that, we don't show our true feelings too much. In our line of work, any hint of vulnerability could get us killed."

If Dad was trying to make her feel better about pursuing

a relationship with Ethan, telling her that falling in love with Ethan could get him killed wasn't the way to go about it.

Whoa, hang on, I am not falling in love with Ethan. Nope. No way. Not happening.

Isabella tried to grasp that thought close, but her heart pushed it away, telling her that yes she was. Nope, she wasn't listening to her heart. This time she was going to listen to her head, and her head said no way.

Why did she think her heart was laughing at her?

"Now I've gone and worried you, haven't I?" he asked.

"No, you haven't." Even she could hear the tremor in her voice.

"That wasn't what I meant to do. Back in my day, things were different from what they are today. I've found that out from my frequent visits to the veterans' home and by talking to this generation of soldiers. Now, the men tell me there's a lot more avenues of support for families and servicemen than before. Places where both men and women can talk about issues. The individual special ops teams are like little communities. All supporting and being there for each other during good times and bad. Certainly makes me wonder if some of the services they talk about were available during my marriage, things may have been different for us." He paused and ran a hand over his head. "Sure, there are still some relationships that don't work out. Hell, I know I should've done more for your mom. You shouldn't have had to deal with what you did as a kid. That's on me. I hold myself accountable for letting you both down."

Tears began a slow trickle down her cheeks. This was the most honest she'd ever heard her father being. The conversation they were now having was one they should've had years ago, when he first moved to San Antonio to be closer to her. "I feel like I should say it's not your fault," she began. "But I'd be lying if I did." God, it killed her to say that to her dad, but honesty was needed in this conversation. To rebuild their relationship, and boy did she want to rebuild it, both of them wouldn't benefit if she denied how she truly felt.

"I wouldn't want you to say that, Isabella, because as you pointed out, it wouldn't be the truth. But I hope that we can move forward. I've missed my daughter even though we live only a half an hour apart. I do understand the distance between us; I deserve your cold shoulder."

Isabella stood and rushed to her dad's seat. He stood and wrapped his arms around her. She laid her head on his chest and inhaled the familiar scent of Old Spice. It was a scent she'd always associated with her dad and had avoided sniffing over the years. Now the smell comforted her as she shed the tears she should've let out many years ago.

"Is everything okay here?" Ethan's voice penetrated her fog.

"Everything is fine," her dad returned as he rubbed his hand over her back. "Isabella and I have sorted out a few issues."

Squeezing her dad one last time, she pulled out of his

hold and faced Ethan. His dark eyes were cloudy with concern, reminding her of his earlier remark about having her six.

She wound her arms around Ethan's waist. "I'm fine, Ethan," she murmured and ran her hands up and down his back. Slowly the tension drained out of him and his arms closed around her. Giving in to the urge that had been inside of her the second he touched her, she laid her head on his chest and sighed.

"I've never liked it when someone cries. I'm sorry for overreacting when I walked in."

"It's okay, and they were cleansing tears. Trust me." Her breath hiccoughed out of her when his thumb swiped away the moisture lingering on her cheek.

Her heart fluttered in her chest and she melted against him even more. Going up on tiptoe she brushed her lips across his, before looking at him, making sure his attention was fully on her and not her dad who still stood behind her.

Once she had Ethan's attention, she said, "I promise you I needed to cry. It's been a long time coming. And I promise you that I truly am fine."

His gaze was immovable, as though he was digging into the far recesses of her mind to reassure himself what she was saying was the truth. Whatever he saw, must have satisfied him because he nodded and dropped another kiss on her nose. "Would you like another beer, Eric?"

Her father barked out a laugh and Ethan's lips stretched

into an answering smile, encouraging her own to lift at the corners. "How about me?" she asked with a wink.

"Would you like one?" Ethan asked picking the small carton he must have placed on the ground when he walked in.

"Absolutely."

While she might have sorted out some of the issues with her father and their relationship was on an even footing at the moment, they still had a long way to go. As she well knew, life could change in a heartbeat.

A FEW HOURS later, Ethan parked his car in her driveway. The rest of the afternoon had gone off so well, they'd ended up staying at her dad's house for dinner.

When they left, he grabbed her in another sweet hug and whispered in her ear, "I love you, honey bee." From memory that was the first time he'd ever said the words to her. She'd been too choked up to return the words, so she'd nodded instead. Now she wished she'd said something like *me too* to him.

"You've been quiet on the drive home. You doing okay?"

"Yeah, I am. Just processing everything that went on to-day. Dad and I made progress. We both have work to do, and I know I have to try harder than I have been." She reached over and squeezed his thigh. "Thanks for coming today. I'm sure it wasn't what you expected."

"I was happy to be there. Although, I may wait before I introduce you to my family. After you meet them, you may kick me to the curb."

She laughed and went to remove her hand, only to have Ethan lay his warm one over hers. Instinct told her he was only joking, but what if there was something bad about his family? Would they not like her because she wasn't in the service? "Why do you say that? Should I be worried?"

He turned his hand beneath hers and entwined their fingers. "Because when I tell them I'm bringing home a girl for Sunday dinner, my parents invite everyone over. It gets loud, and they're all big huggers. Also, I'm an only child; my parents think I can do no wrong. Which is totally right, of course." He winked.

Isabella rolled her eyes. "If I can handle a room full of unruly fifth graders who *think* they know everything, I can deal with your family."

"We'll see." He chuckled, lifted their co-joined hands, and placed a kiss on her fingers.

Her breath caught in her throat and desire for Ethan simmered to life inside of her. Being with him tonight, kissing every inch of his body would be the perfect way to end the evening. "Do you want to come in?" she asked, breathless from the merest of touches.

"I'd love to, but I can't. I need to get back home, I have PT first thing and it's better if I'm home."

"BACK TO THE real world, huh?" she tried to joke, but it fell flatter than a pancake.

"Unfortunately, and I don't know if I'm going to be able to see you this week. We've got a lot of training exercises to go through because I'll be deploying again soon."

And there it was, the two words she hadn't wanted to think about or let enter her mind—deployment and training. Words she couldn't avoid if she wanted to move forward in her life with Ethan by her side. And she did, but it was so easy to cling to what made her comfortable, even if it was unhealthy. To fall back into the safety of thinking the worst would happen to those she cared about.

The reality of the situation was, their relationship was so new, and even with the support of her dad and the people she'd meet on the weekend, could she and Ethan really survive an extended absence after only knowing each other for a few weeks?

A hand closed around her head and pulled her gently toward him. Resisting the lure was useless; she wanted to be as close to him as she could. "We'll be fine, Izzy. You don't know how much I want to be able to take you inside and worship you. But I do need to get back home."

With one of her hands still tangled up in his, she placed her free hand on his cheek. "It's okay, I understand." And she did, even if she didn't want to. She closed the gap and kissed him, hoping to convey all that she was feeling through her kiss.

His lips moved over hers, eliciting a moan from her. His tongue delved into her mouth deepening the kiss. She didn't know how long they were connected but the need to breathe had her pulling her lips away from his.

"Let me walk you to your door," he murmured.

"I'd like that."

With another peck on her lips, he released her and opened his door. He was around her side of the car in a flash. A few moments later they were standing at her door, her key in her hand.

"Thank you for today, Ethan. I'm glad you came with me."

"As I said, I had a wonderful time. I like your dad."

She smiled. "He likes you too."

"Phew," he responded wiping his hand across his forehead in an exaggerated movement. "That's a relief."

"Oh, please, there were times you two completely forgot I was in the room when you started talking guns and stuff," she teased, punching him lightly on the arm.

He captured her hand and tugged her so she fell against his chest. "I never forgot where you were, Izzy. You're unforgettable to me."

His lips captured hers again in a fierce, erotic kiss. Spindles of desire entwined around her heart and she groaned against his mouth while grinding her lower body against his growing erection.

"Are you sure I can't tempt you to stay? Even for a little bit?" she asked.

"God, I wish I could say yes, but I can't." He tempered his rejection with another evocative kiss, she wouldn't be surprised that one day she'd climax just from his lips on hers.

The reluctance to end the embrace between them wasn't fake, she felt it as much as he did. Taking a deep breath, she inserted her key in the lock. Before she could twist it open, Ethan's warm hand closed over hers. "Let me."

He twisted the key and opened the door, stepping over the threshold before her. "What are you doing?" she asked, trying not to get her hopes up that he had changed his mind about spending the night with her.

"Making sure your house is fine."

"Seriously? Didn't we already have this discussion when you left? I don't need you to do this, Ethan." Isabella grabbed his arm to halt his progress. Normally if she went out she'd always leave a light on in case it was dark when she got home. Because she hadn't expected the lunch with her dad to trail into dinner, she hadn't bothered to leave one on. "You do know I come home to an empty house all the time?"

"Yes, but that was before I knew you. Now that I do, I'm going to worry every time you come home."

"Well, this isn't going to work for me. But how about I send you a text every time I get home so you know I'm okay?" Compromise was everything in a relationship.

"That would make me very happy." He looked at his watch and groaned. "I really need to go."

He swept her close again for another kiss.

"You'll never leave if you keep doing that," she said breathlessly a few minutes later.

Ethan chuckled and smoothed a hand down her back. "You are simply irresistible, Isabella Knowles."

"Likewise, Ethan Masters, but I won't be blamed for you having to do an extra hundred push-ups because you were dragging your ass at PT."

"Oh, you wound me." He winked at her and turned to walk to her door.

Isabella followed behind, dragging her feet because she really didn't want to say goodbye to him. He got to the door and opened it, waiting for her to catch up with him.

"I'll try to call when I can," he said and dropped a kiss on her nose.

"Sounds good." With one last lingering look, he turned on his heel and headed to his car. So this was what it was going to be like, watching him leave whenever he was deployed. Following his retreating back as he walked onto a plane or into a car. It was going to be hard, but she'd do it.

Chapter Thirteen

ETHAN GLANCED AT his phone, trying to see if he could get any signal. The chances of that happening were going to be slim. They were doing a training exercise in the middle of nowhere Texas. The sun was beating down unrelentingly on his back. Sam was panting beside him and all he wanted to do was sink into the coldest vat of water possible. That wasn't going to happen for another three days.

"Put the phone away, before the chief master sergeant sees you. I can't believe you didn't hand your phone over," Zeke hissed.

"You can't tell me you haven't been trying to get signal?" he retorted.

"Well, yeah, but Anna's about to have our first baby. I like to think if I get caught, I've got a justifiable excuse. You on the other hand, don't."

Zeke was right, but part of him needed to let Isabella know everything was okay. This was his first away training assignment, and given her past history with her husband, the need to reassure her was strong. It had been almost a month since their weekend together. They'd gone on a few dates and he'd spent as much time as he could with her and in her bed.

Just thinking about her lying sprawled across her sheets, her hair spread over her pillow, her lips parted, tempting him to taste them, had his body twitching against his pants.

"This is the first time I've been away from Izzy for any length of time without contact." No way could Ethan tell Zeke about Isabella's first marriage and what happened to her husband. He couldn't help but worry about how she was dealing with him being away. He'd met her friend Meredith and she would be there for Izzy if she needed support. So would her father. "I'm worried that's all. I know you probably went through this when you began dating Anna."

Zeke ran a cloth across his sweaty forehead. "Yeah, but I know Anna said she'd keep in touch with Isabella, let her know she wasn't alone while we were away. That's what Patricia did with Anna, so Anna now wants to pay it forward for Isabella."

"Thanks, man, I appreciate it." He suspected as much but didn't want to assume Anna and the others would be there for Isabella.

"Hey, you know we all look out for each other, that includes our women. Come on, we're being summoned." Zeke canted his head to the left and Ethan saw his superior officer signaling them to come over to him.

"Let's go, Sam," he said, and his partner stood up ready for her next instruction from him. "Thanks for the chat,

Zeke, I needed it."

"Anytime."

Once they reached the chief master sergeant, he looked up and zeroed in on Zeke. "Hopkins, I've just received notification your wife has gone into labor. Seeing as we've done the major training drills today, I'm granting you permission to go to her. A helo has been dispatched and is set to arrive in thirty minutes."

The color drained from his friend's face and Ethan relinquished his hold on Sam to steady the man.

"Fuck, I'm about to become a dad." There was an incredulous note in his voice and Ethan laughed.

"Yep, sure sounds like it. Congrats, man, that's awesome."

"I don't know if I can do this. What sort of dad am I going to be?"

"An awesome one, so stop fucking about and get your shit together so you're ready to go when the 'copter arrives."

Zeke swallowed and nodded as a hint of color returned back to his face. "Yeah, you're right."

"When am I ever wrong?" Ethan joked.

That got an eye roll from his friend. "All the fucking time." Zeke then turned to the gathered men and yelled, "I'm gonna be a fucking dad."

Everyone laughed and wished him well. A tinge of envy spiked through Ethan. Prior to meeting Isabella thoughts of becoming a father had been a far off dream. Now that he had, he couldn't get pictures of Isabella round with their baby, out of his mind. Her lying in a hospital bed clasping a tiny bundle, her eyes alight with joy and glistening with tears.

Damn, he wanted to make those images come true. The bigger question was, would Izzy want this—with him?

WALKING INTO HIS house, Ethan dumped his pack on the ground and leaned back against the door, closing his eyes. Exhaustion lined every single muscle and bone in his body. All he wanted to do was take a shower and collapse on his bed. He'd received a phone call from Lieutenant Colonial Blue when he arrived back at base, asking him if he'd made any decisions about his reenlistment and promotion. He'd been avoiding thinking about it and he hadn't spoken to Isabella either. He needed to talk to her soon. He didn't understand his reticence in bringing the subject up.

Yes you do. You're worried she's going to ask you to give it all away and you don't want to.

He sighed, he wasn't up for a mental argument, no matter how much truth there was in his internal thoughts.

Later.

He took a deep breath and held it.

What?

He took another deep breath. Nope he hadn't been imagining it, he could smell wildflowers. The same scent he always smelled when he was with Isabella. She'd only been to his house once, and that was a couple of days after the weekend they'd first made love. He'd spent most of his time at her place because Caleb was still seeing Amy.

The only reason he was smelling her scent was because he was tired and she'd been on his mind most of his trip. It was amazing he'd got through his exercises; his mind hadn't been totally focused on the job.

"Hey, soldier boy."

Now he was imaging hearing her. He really was tired. With a sigh, he pulled himself away from the door as he opened his eyes. His step faltered when he clapped eyes on the vision in front of him.

And what a vision it was. No way was his Isabella standing in the hallway of his house. It just wasn't possible, because he hadn't told her when and what time he'd be returning, and she didn't have a key to his house.

Just to make sure there weren't any doubts, he rubbed his eyes. When he opened them again there she stood, all beautiful in one of the maxi dresses she liked to wear in summer, her blonde hair curled over her shoulders and a big smile on her face.

"Airman, not soldier boy."

"Well, then, hey, airman."

Ethan was half convinced he'd fallen asleep standing up. "You're real?"

She laughed and glided toward him. "Very real."

Ethan reached out to clasp her hands when she went to hug him. "God, Izzy, as much as I want to hold you, I'm covered in dirt and shit and stink to high heaven."

A serene smile crossed her face. "I don't care. I missed you." Seconds later she closed the distance and kissed him soundly on his lips. Groaning, Ethan wrapped his arms around her and pulled her tight against him.

Every night while he was away, he dreamed about holding her. Kissing her the way he was kissing her right now. Reality was so much better than dreams.

His body hardened with every passing second their lips roamed over each other. He'd like nothing more than to lay her on the hardwood floor and ravish her, but he really didn't want to transfer any of his five-day trip on her. Pulling his lips away, he rested his chin on top of her head. "Now this is a welcome home I could definitely get used to. How did you know when I would be getting home? How did you get in?"

Isabella laughed and then her nose crinkled. "Boy, you weren't wrong, you really do stink."

"Hey." He took a step away, colliding with the front door again, and held up his hands in a surrender motion. "I warned you, but you said you didn't care."

She smiled another soft smile and raised her hand to rest it lightly against his five-day growth. "It was worth it, but I think you need to take a shower. And I need to check dinner.

When we're eating, I'll answer all your questions." Going on tiptoe she kissed him on his nose, before turning and striding down the hallway, her skirt swishing around her ankles. She might be covered from the tops of her breasts to her ankles, but damn, it was sexy as sin. He knew exactly what lay beneath that fabric and he couldn't wait to get his hands on her.

Half an hour later, he strode down the hallway toward the kitchen. He'd raced through his shower because all he wanted to do was be with Izzy. Now he understood what the guys were talking about when they said coming home to a woman was the best feeling in the world. He always thought they were exaggerating but seeing Isabella standing in his hallway, waiting for him to arrive home, had surpassed anything he'd ever felt in his life. What he wanted most was to ensure that it happened all the time, but he was getting ahead of himself. They'd only been dating seriously for a month; it was way too soon to be thinking of forever. There was still too much to work through before any talk of love.

Halting the runaway train his thoughts had boarded seemed impossible when he walked into the kitchen as Isabella pulled a steaming dish out of the oven. A delicious, spicy aroma enveloped the kitchen and his stomach grumbled appreciatively. "Please tell me you made me your amazing lasagna?"

The dish clattered to the stove top and he cringed at the sound. "Geez, Ethan, you could've warned me you'd come into the kitchen."

There was no heat in her words indicating she wasn't too upset with him. He sidled up to her, hooked an arm around her waist, and looked down at the dish. His stomach grumbled again when he spied the neatly layered pasta covered in a red sauce and bubbling melted cheese. "You did. You are a goddess." He dropped a kiss on the back of her neck, enjoying the shiver that rippled through her. "I lo—uh can't wait to taste it."

What the hell? Was he about to say he loved her? Hadn't he just lectured himself that it was too soon to be thinking beyond the here and now with Isabella? He was exhausted after an intense week; after a good night's sleep everything would make sense.

"I set the table in your dining room, why don't you go in there and I'll bring everything in."

Glad to get away so he could get his wayward thoughts under control, Ethan mumbled what he hoped sounded like an *okay* and exited the kitchen.

When he walked into the dining room he stopped dead. The table that was usually covered with junk now sported a pale yellow tablecloth. A vase of brightly colored flowers sat in the middle. The silverware sparkled beneath the chandelier and he wondered if she'd polished them before laying them down. His mismatched plates looked out of place in such an elegant setting but his heart took another running leap into the well of love at the effort she put in to make his welcome home a memorable one.

"Excuse me," Isabella murmured as she walked into the room. He took a side step, still unable to believe he wasn't dreaming all of this.

"I can't believe you went to all this trouble, for me." He laid a hand on Izzy's arm as she walked past him. "Why?"

The confidence that had been sparkling in her gorgeous blue eyes dimmed a little and he felt like an ass for causing it. Her tongue darted out and swiped across her bottom lip, the action went straight to his groin, hardening his dick against his jeans. "Because I missed you."

As hungry as he was, the words she spoke pierced his heart and he gathered her close. His need for her overriding everything else. "God, I missed you too," he whispered before he bent and scooped her up in his arms.

"Ethan," she squeaked out in shock. "Dinner's going to get cold."

"I don't care, I want you far more than I want to eat." He pressed a kiss against her cheek and walked out of the dining room, heading for his room instead.

Thank God, for his air force training. His bedroom was spic and span clean. He'd dumped his backpack in the laundry before his shower and his dirty uniform was hidden in the hamper in the bathroom.

Gently, he laid her down on the bed, following so he was beside her. He traced a finger over her face. "I dreamed about you every night I was away, but not once did I dream that you'd be waiting for me when I walked through the door."

He captured her lips, preventing her from responding. He really didn't want to talk, all he wanted to do was make love to this beautiful woman and claim her as his own.

ISABELLA STIRRED, OPENING her eyes to an unfamiliar room. Something had woken her but she didn't know what. She stretched and the sheet drifted a little lower on her naked skin.

Naked skin? I don't sleep naked.

A warm hand drifted across her belly. "Hey, honey."

Her body shivered in response to Ethan's softly spoken words. Everything came back to her. Her surprising him on his return from training trip. Him scooping her up and making love to her so exquisitely she'd cried. Them eating dinner in bed, before they feasted on each other again.

"Hey, yourself. Did I wake you?" she asked trying to see if she could see the time. "What's the time?"

"Just before five."

She groaned, she never woke up that early. Then again, waking up next to a hunk of a man, a man she could no longer deny was becoming important to her, was new to her too.

No way would she tell Ethan about her feelings. Expressing them out loud would likely put a jinx on whatever was growing between them and that was the last thing she wanted to do. While he'd been away, Anna had had her baby and when she'd gone to see the other woman, Zeke had been there all proud father. Her step had faltered because in her mind she imagined it was her and Ethan in the hospital holding their own baby. How she'd gotten through the visit she didn't know but she had.

Perhaps it had been something on her face that she hadn't been able to hide, but Anna had seen it because when she'd received a call from the other woman telling her when Ethan would be home and that Caleb had left a spare key under the obligatory flower pot, she stopped thinking and had only acted.

Now her actions had landed her in his bed and, for once, she didn't regret her spontaneity.

"Did you fall asleep on me again?"

Isabella grabbed the sheet and pulled it up, turning so the hand Ethan had resting on her belly slid around to her back. She wiggled closer to him, his erection nudging her belly. "No, and I can see you're not sleepy either."

Ethan chuckled and nuzzled her neck. "I'm used to waking early."

She ran a hand over his warm chest and down his back. "Do you have to go to PT today?" she asked, dreading the answer to that question. It was Saturday and she wanted to spend the day in his bed.

"Nope, not today. We have the weekend off for a change."

"Good." With a shove against his shoulder he fell back against the mattress and she straddled him. "I've got plans for you Mr. Masters."

"That's Master Sergeant Masters to you, ma'am."

Her heart fluttered. It was the first time he'd referred to himself by his rank and some of the fears she'd being carrying around with her since they'd started dating resurfaced. With a concerted effort, she pushed them down.

No, this time was for them. She wasn't going to let real life intrude on this moment. Oh, she couldn't ignore it forever, but for a little while she planned to.

Lowering her head she trailed her mouth along his collarbone before finding his nipple and swirling her tongue around the small disk. His groan rumbled through his chest and vibrated against her cheek. Her lips ventured further down and when she reached his erection, she kissed the tip of it. In answer to her seeking tongue, his fingers threaded through her hair. There was a slight pull of pain but she didn't mind. It was his turn to experience the pleasure he'd given her multiple times during the night.

Her tongue traced down his hard length before sliding back up to swirl around the head of his dick. His moan encouraged her. She opened her lips and closed over him, sucking him deep into her mouth.

"Jesus, Izzy, that feels amazing." He moaned low and

long.

Hearing his sounds of pleasure empowered her and she increased her pace. Just when she was getting into a good rhythm, Ethan pulled his fingers from her hair and lifted her head away from him. She let him go with a pop.

Before she could ask him what was wrong he hauled her up his chest and devoured her mouth with his. His arms banded around her, holding her tight against his chest. She reveled in the contact, sure she would never get enough of it.

He broke their kiss and rubbed his cheek against hers. "This is the best way to wake up."

"I can't complain about it either," she managed to get out before her lips were captured again.

She ran her hands down his side, clutching his waist to keep him close to her. She ground her hips against his erection, telling him in no uncertain terms what she wanted.

In a flash, she was flipped over and Ethan propped himself up on his hands, looking down at her. "You are so beautiful, Izzy. I can't believe you're here in my bed."

Reaching up, she cupped his cheek. "I am, and I have no plans to be anywhere else today."

"Thank God," he said as he lowered the bottom half of his body against her, his erection nudging her entrance.

All it would take would be a lift of her hips and he would be able to slide right into her. She was so ready for him. As if sensing her thoughts, Ethan placed a hand on her hip stilling her movement. With his other he reached over and retrieved another condom from the bedside table.

His lips kissed her gently as he dealt with protection and when he thrust his tongue inside of her, he entered her at the same time.

She ripped her mouth away from his. "I've never felt anything like this before." She cried out as he began to move slowly within her. She was so worked up from having him in her mouth and their kisses that she didn't want to take it slow. She wanted him to take her hard and fast.

When she tried to increase the pace, his fingers tightened around her waist, holding her in place so he could keep the tempo of their lovemaking to his liking.

"I need you to go faster," she whispered against his shoulder.

His lips brushed her ear. "Normally, I'd grant you your wish, but not now. I'm savoring every inch of you and every moment."

She sighed and turned her head allowing their lips to meld together in an evocative kiss. As his body continued to move in her and his lips and tongue caressed her mouth, sensations like she'd never experienced before built inside of her, coalescing at the juncture of her thighs before spreading out and consuming her as her orgasm crashed through her. Her inner muscles vibrated against his dick and finally, his thrusts became faster and soon he was crying out her name. It was the most intense orgasm she'd ever had in her life and her body still shook in reaction to it.

Ethan collapsed on top of her, his chest heaving in and out against her breasts. "Izzy," he whispered.

He didn't need to say anything more, she knew exactly what he meant. Their relationship had taken another turn and she, for one, couldn't wait to keep traveling down the road with him.

Chapter Fourteen

ETHAN GAVE SAM one last pat on the head before he straightened. He looked around the kennel area and tried to imagine himself managing it all. The thought of not working day in and day out with Sam cut deep. She was like an extra limb; without her, he'd be lost.

He'd discussed the promotion with his parents, who were proud of him and told him he had to go for it, that if he wanted to progress in his career then it was a moot point.

What he hadn't told them was about his indecision whether he would sign his reenlistment papers or not. Both his parents assumed he'd do his twenty and then retire and find a job using the skills he'd learned.

He couldn't deny that had been his plan all along, but now he wanted to discuss his future with Isabella.

Therein lay the problem. Would he, or could he, give up the life he'd imagined himself having since he was a kid, for her? He was five years away from his twenty years. He was up for a promotion that would benefit his skill set. The desire to serve and protect his country hadn't died since he'd met Isabella.

"Masters, are you listening to me?"

Lost in his thoughts, Ethan hadn't noticed Lieutenant Colonel Blue standing beside him.

"Sir," he said and stood to attention. "I apologize. I didn't hear what you said."

A rare smile broke out over his superior officer's face. "I suspected as much. I wanted to see if you'd given any thought on our discussion last month."

Was the man psychic? "I was just thinking about it, sir."

Blue nodded and crossed his arms over his chest. "Good. I don't want to pressure you or anything, but we can't afford to lose airmen like you. Your record is impeccable and so is your commitment to the force and your squadron. You will always be a valuable member whether you're first in or training the dogs to protect our men. Remember that when you're considering the promotion and your reenlistment while you're deployed."

"Thank you, sir."

"Enjoy your evening and weekend, Masters."

Blue walked away, leaving Ethan to consider his words. Being in the K-9 division of the security forces for many years, he was well aware of the role the kennel master played. In his gut, he knew the role was important, not only to the K-9 officers but to the rest of the squadron as well. If he did take the promotion, he'd still be an integral part of his group. Still be responsible for the safety of the other guys, just in a different capacity.

He could no longer avoid talking to Isabella about it. He wanted a future with her, but he wouldn't compromise his career. When the time came, he would sign the papers for another go-around. After he'd completed his required years, then he would seriously consider retirement. He was sure he and Isabella could come to a place where both their needs were met.

At least he hoped they could.

So MANY THOUGHTS swirled around Ethan's mind as he drove up Isabella's driveway. He'd been tempted to cancel on her until he got his thoughts straightened out into some sort of order. But, there was so much they needed to discuss. He had to explain his future career path and desires. The question was, how would she take his news? Would she encourage him to take the promotion? They'd also not discussed his upcoming deployment. She always tried to change the subject on him. Would she break it off with him, saying she really couldn't cope knowing he planned to stay in the armed forces for at least another five years and would be deployed during that time too?

Dammit, he needed to stop, he'd been on this same thought roller coaster since he'd left the base.

He pulled to a stop behind a car he didn't recognize. Had they made plans with another couple tonight and he'd forgotten? He didn't think so.

Grabbing his overnight bag from the passenger seat, he got out and strode up to the front door. Normally he'd let himself in with the key Izzy had given him, but if they had a guest he didn't want to just barge in.

Stupid thought really, considering how much time he'd spent there over the last month, but he just felt he needed to knock on the door tonight.

Before he could raise his fist, the door opened and an annoyed-looking Isabella answered.

"Oh, God, Ethan, I'm so sorry my dad's here. He just turned up out of the blue. He doesn't do this."

Dropping his bag on the ground he reached out and pulled Isabella close to him, not quite understanding her issue with her dad being at her house. He ran a hand up and down her back, hoping to soothe her anxiety. Once he could tell her breathing had calmed down a little, he pulled back and placed a soft, chaste kiss on her lips. "Want to tell me what the problem is with your dad turning up unannounced?"

"He brought a woman with him. He thought it was time I met his girlfriend. I didn't even know Dad had a girlfriend. We've been mending our relationship ever since that day at his place when you first met him. Not once has he mentioned he had a girlfriend. I'm so angry that he didn't trust me with this. It's important information."

Ahh, there it was, the trust issue between Isabella and her

dad. He could understand why she'd be feeling so hurt. But he also understood why Eric had kept things quiet. Ethan imagined Eric wanted to make sure his relationship with his daughter was on solid ground before he introduced another facet to their dynamic.

"Honey, just like that Sunday when I met your dad for the first time, I have your back. I'll support you and if you want them to leave I'll ask Eric to leave. Explain how you're feeling. I'm sure he didn't keep his girlfriend from you to be malicious. I think he was so keen to fix things with you that that was his focus."

"These two situations are not the same at all. He at least knew you existed when you met him. I don't know anything about this woman."

"Our circumstances were different, your dad set us up on a blind date. He wanted to see if the guy Lincoln had said was perfect for his daughter actually was." Ethan hooked a finger under her chin and raised her face. "And I am, you know. I am perfect for you."

Time stood still as their eyes said the words both were afraid to speak out loud. Ethan hoped he conveyed how important Isabella was to him and that no matter what, he would always be there for her.

"Honey bee, why did you rush off like that? Oh, Ethan, I didn't know you were coming over." He must have spied the bag on the floor. "Hmm, seems you're here for a couple of days too."

There wasn't disapproval in Eric's voice, but maybe just a little bit of protective father coming out. Regardless of the fact that his daughter was a grown woman, Eric would be a father first and foremost, even if Isabella didn't believe they had that sort of relationship.

Placing another kiss on Isabella's forehead, he released his arms and closed the distance between him and the other man. "Eric, it's good to see you. I understand you brought a friend with you."

Out of the corner of his eye, he spied Isabella's back straightening. Okay, he'd overstepped his mark, but if Eric wanted to play protective father, he was going to play concerned and caring boyfriend. Actually, it wasn't playing at all, he was both and more when it came to Isabella. He would be her champion, no matter what the fallout.

Eric studied Ethan and he stood still, meeting the other man's gaze head-on.

A slow smile stretched across Eric's face. "Yes, yes I did. I suppose I should've called her instead of dropping in unannounced."

"You don't say," Isabella muttered.

For an ex-soldier who'd worked in special forces, like Eric had, for him to admit he was wrong, was huge. Through a short conversation an understanding had been reached. Eric was now aware his daughter wasn't alone anymore, and Ethan understood the gift he'd been given.

"But, Ethan, you do anything to hurt her, and it will be

the last mistake you ever make." There it was—the merce-
nary soldier who took no prisoners. Ethan respected Eric's
comment, and if roles were reversed and he had a daughter
he'd do the same.

"Understood, sir." He would do everything in his power
not to hurt her, but with the subjects he needed to address,
he couldn't guarantee there wouldn't be some hurt in the
future—for both of them.

"Would anyone like to clue me on what the hell just
happened? I feel like there was a lot of unspoken words and
I've been auctioned off to the highest bidder," Isabella asked,
moving so she was in between him and Eric. "This is the
twenty-first century, you know. I'm not a commodity for
both of you to put on a shelf and say *there, there* when I'm
upset. I didn't take you to task when you arrived, Dad,
because I didn't want to appear rude. Maybe I should have.
But you could've told me about Rhonda. I'm not a little girl
anymore. I'm okay with you moving on with your life." She
paused. "And you, Ethan"—she poked his finger in his
chest—"I don't need you to go all *airman* on me with my
father. I can do that myself. Yes, I may have answered the
door upset, but I'm allowed to."

She had her hands on her hips and her eyes blazed with
annoyance and, perhaps, a hint of pride. She'd never looked
sexier and he tempered his urge to scoop her up and take her
against the hallway wall. Now that would be a good impression to make. He liked seeing this strong, confident Isabella.

If only she believed in her inner strength.

"You're right. I'm sorry, but I'm not going to apologize for protecting you. I know I've said it all before, and I'm sure your dad is the same—we're trained to protect those we care about. It's hard to shut off."

"It's true, Isabella, it is hard to turn off," her dad added. "And I'm sorry for not being honest and upfront with you about Rhonda. You're right, we've had enough conversations over the past month for me to bring it up."

"Good. Now if you'll excuse me, I'm going to check on dinner." She swiveled and strode down the hallway.

As he watched her retreating back, he smiled. God, he loved her. The smile died as he let the thought take hold, dig its root into his heart, and, instead of scaring the shit out of him, peace settled over him.

He loved her.

There was no point in denying it any longer. He wanted to spend the rest of his life with her, but he wasn't sure Isabella was there with him. The last thing he wanted to do was frighten her away by declaring his emotions, not to mention the fact he was about to leave for an overseas stint and he wanted to talk to her about his promotion.

Maybe it was best he kept that bit of news to himself. Get her prepared for the idea of him leaving and when she was comfortable with that, tell her about the promotion.

"I hope you know what you're doing, Ethan."

Lost in the realization that he loved Isabella, he'd forgotten her dad was still standing near him.

Like all good special forces personnel, Ethan had no doubt Eric studied his body language and the emotions flitting across his face. In normal circumstances Ethan would've ensured that he'd kept his thoughts and feelings hidden. Showing vulnerabilities could lead to death.

The last thing he needed to do, though, was to give Isabella's father a reason to doubt his faith in Ethan that he would cherish and protect Isabella. "Yes, Eric, I do."

ISABELLA CLOSED THE door on her dad and his girlfriend, glad the evening was over.

"After a shaky start, it ended up being a good evening, right?"

She swiveled and spied Ethan leaning against the doorway of the living room and hallway. God, he looked so sexy casually standing there, a glass of red wine in his hand. After the *discussion* between him and her father when he first arrived, Ethan had been the perfect boyfriend. Courteous, making jokes with Rhonda, and making the other woman feel comfortable.

She sighed and walked toward him, welcoming the embrace he offered. "I was pretty rude to Rhonda when she first arrived. It wasn't my finest moment."

"Come on, let's go sit." He led her into the living room

and settled her on the couch. He placed his wineglass on the table and then came to sit beside her, arranging them so he was lying and his back rested against the cushions, she was tucked up with his hard chest to her back.

Another sigh rippled through her. This felt so right, the two of them lying on her couch, not saying anything but a million words seemed to fill the silence.

"Want to tell me all that happened before I arrived?" he prodded her gently.

"When the doorbell rang I thought it was you. I opened the door and was about to admonish you for losing your key when I saw Dad and Rhonda standing on my front porch. Shock is a poor word for the emotion that slammed into me. I felt betrayed."

"Why, Izzy?"

"Because I could tell from the way they were standing that this wasn't a new thing between the two of them. There was a comfortableness about them that can only come from when you spend a lot of time with the other person. Dad and I have been speaking on a regular basis. Heck, we've even gone out for dinner and I've been over to his place numerous times and he didn't mention her even once. It brought back all the memories of when I kept things from him and he kept things from me. I thought our relationship had progressed and then he turns up with a woman he's never uttered a word about. At least Dad admitted he was wrong about it all."

"Well, you made it clear to him how you felt. I don't think he'll be making that mistake again."

"Yep, another step forward in our relationship."

"I know now that in some situations I can't take over and need to let you take charge."

"I'm sure there will be some situations where I'll be okay with you taking charge." If she was in physical danger, she'd be glad to have him by her side. But when it came to situations with her father, well, it was up to her to deal with them.

"I got the message loud and clear. I'm sorry I overstepped, but I did it because I care."

Memories of the way he looked at her earlier in the evening came rushing back. The intense look of desire burning in the depths of dark brown eyes. Heat flared through her body.

Facing him, she framed his face with her hands. "I know. I'm beginning to understand that about you and know that sometimes you can't help it. Doesn't mean I'll let you run roughshod over me all the time."

Ethan laughed and placed his hands over hers. "I wouldn't expect anything less."

She was done talking. She wanted to lose herself in her man's arms and spend the night in a passion-filled fog.

Leaning forward, she closed her lips over his, communicating her needs and desires in her kiss. Ethan answered her call and, in that moment, everything in her life was perfect.

Chapter Fifteen

ISABELLA LOWERED THE paper she'd been grading when she heard Ethan pad into the kitchen. His hair was mussed and, in his boxers, he looked so sexy she wanted to jump him right there and then. Only she'd kept him busy the previous evening. It had been late when they'd finally fallen into a passion-soaked sleep.

When the alarm went off at five for him to get up to go for a run, he'd slammed his hand on her clock and rolled over and promptly fell back asleep. For her, on the other hand, sleep had been fitful and at seven she gave up trying to get any. Besides, she had some papers to grade. Summer was coming up fast and keeping the kids focused was as challenging as keeping herself focused.

"Hey, airman, how'd you sleep?"

"Not long enough," he grumbled.

Now this was interesting. Even when he had little sleep, Ethan always seemed perky in the morning. Pushing back from the table, she walked over to where he stood by the fridge drinking the glass of water he'd just poured.

"Are you feeling okay?" She went to lay a hand on his

forehead when it was captured in one of his hands. The action pulled her forward and she splayed her palms against his warm, naked, chest to stop from crashing fully into him.

"No, I'm not feeling okay. I woke up and you weren't there. I didn't like it."

For a split second she stood stock still, not sure what to think then she started laughing. "Oh, you poor baby. I couldn't sleep so I decided to not disturb you with my tossing and turning. Besides, I had some marking I wanted to finish up."

"Well, if you have trouble sleeping, I'm sure I could've come up with a way to help you." He ground his hips against hers and there was no way she could miss his erection.

A shiver of desire rippled through her. After the night they'd spent together worshiping each other's bodies, their libidos should've been sated, but hers was as fired up as his was.

Wrapping her arms around his neck, she went up on tip-toe and nipped at his lips. "I don't have to be anywhere today and you told me you don't either, so we could go back to bed if you like. I'm feeling a little tired now and could probably do with some more sleep." She faked a yawn to get her point across.

Ethan lifted her, and she hooked her legs around his waist. "Is that right?" he asked as he steered them out of the kitchen and back in the direction of her bedroom.

"Yes, it is."

"Well, let me help you sleep then," he said as he lowered his head and kissed any rational thoughts out of her mind.

ISABELLA SNUGGLED INTO Ethan's embrace enjoying the post-coital lethargy that enveloped them both.

"I need to talk to you about something," Ethan said as he feathered his fingers up and down her arm.

Muscles that were, only seconds ago, languid and relaxed tensed with the underlying timbre of his voice. Instinctively, Isabella knew exactly what he wanted to talk to her about. Over the last few weeks, he'd tried broaching the subject of his pending deployment, but she'd redirected the conversation every time. She'd handled the news of him having training exercises a little easier. He'd always called her when he could when he'd finished. Communication between them would be difficult while he was deployed.

They couldn't avoid his deployment forever and it seemed that the time had come and avoiding it was no longer a viable option for her.

Pulling away from him was akin to cutting off a piece of her heart, but she needed to have some distance between them when they had this conversation. She sat up against the headboard and hugged her raised knees. A defensive and protective pose if there ever was one but she didn't care. "What did you want to talk about?" she asked, pleased her voice sounded strong, even though inside she was a quivering mass of jelly.

"Izzy, this conversation isn't easy for me either. I've never had to have one like this before, and I don't know how to approach the subject. But every day we avoid it, the closer the deadline approaches, and it becomes bigger than it needs to be."

Yep, he was talking about his pending deployment. There had been talk all those weeks ago at Anna's place about the plans the girls were going to make when their partners and spouses left. She'd been an ostrich and had buried her head in the sand, tuning out the conversation because she didn't think it would matter to her. Or more importantly, it was a topic she didn't want to face.

"When do you leave?" Like ripping off a Band-Aid, ask the question she really didn't want the answer to, but she needed to know.

"In four weeks."

Four weeks!

School let out in three, at least if she had her job she'd be able to attempt to keep her focus on something, but going into an almost three-month summer break, it would be impossible not to constantly worry about him and his squadron.

"How long will you be gone?"

"It depends, it could be a minimum of three months or a maximum of six."

When she'd been married to Travis, she'd never had to deal with him being deployed. He'd died before he ever got his first orders. When she'd been eighteen and young, she'd always believed she could cope with it. She'd been naïve about it all, living in a romantic bubble where nothing could touch her. Now that she was older, the realities of going to a war zone weren't romantic at all.

The realities of being in a relationship with Ethan came crashing in on her.

Six months. A half a year.

But he said it could be as short as three months. Her whole summer. When he returned, she'd be going back to school. Part of her had hoped that something would change, and he wouldn't have to go and they could spend time together over the summer, where she didn't have to worry about lesson plans and maybe he could take a few days off and they could've gone away somewhere.

She'd been living in a fool's paradise to think that was even possible.

"Tell me what you're thinking, Izzy. Don't shut me out now," he pleaded with her but, at the moment, her vocal chords were paralyzed and speaking was impossible.

Making herself swallow a couple of times seemed to dislodge the lump but tears threatened and the last thing she wanted to do was cry in front of him. "I don't know what to say, Ethan. I knew it was coming, but as you know, I'm really good with hiding from things I don't want to face. You going away is one of those things."

The need for space, for some alone time to think over-whelmed her. She needed to get out of this room and this bed, being so close to Ethan was messing with her brain. She threw back the covers, grabbed her robe, and walked out the door, shoving her arms into the silky fabric as she went.

ETHAN SWORE UNDER his breath and reached down to grab the boxers he'd shucked not long ago.

Dammit, why is this so hard?

Because he'd never left the woman he loved behind be-fore. He'd never deployed while in a relationship. Most of his liaisons had been casual and scratched the itch. None of the girls he'd slept with meant as much to him as Isabella did.

It wasn't only his deployment they had to talk about. How could he dump so much information on her at once? After the conversations they'd had last night and the situa-tion with her father, not telling her everything was the same as what her father had done. He couldn't do that to her. It wouldn't be fair.

Running a hand through his hair, he knew what he needed to do; just making his feet walk out the door to find her was proving difficult. Just like when he walked into an unknown situation while deployed, talking about all their issues was a risk he needed to take because maybe he'd be surprised and things would work out for them. Plus, if their relationship lasted this first deployment, there'd be a lot of things they'd have to discuss and not brush aside.

He made sure he was fully dressed this time when he set out to find her, not that he regretted what they'd shared the last hour.

The first room he checked was the kitchen, the papers she'd been working on when he'd previously walked in were still scattered on the table. Even his glass remained on the counter beside the refrigerator. He didn't think she'd have gone for a walk seeing as she was only dressed in her robe, but he strode down the hallway, out the door, and down the path. When he reached the edge of her property, he looked in both directions but couldn't see her. Her car was still in the driveway, not that she could've got out anyway as his car was parked behind hers.

Cursing under his breath, he headed back inside. As he passed the living room he noticed it was empty too.

"Where the hell are you, Izzy?" he murmured as he opened the doors to the spare rooms. She couldn't have just disappeared.

Ethan stopped in his mad search and took a deep breath. He needed to approach this logically, like he would when he was approaching a building and it required him and Sam to search before the others on his team followed. He'd searched the most logical places. If it was him, where would he go where there was space and he wouldn't get interrupted?

Well, he'd go for a walk and seeing as he'd already looked down the street and considering what she'd been wearing when she'd walked out of the bedroom, he could scratch that off his list.

"Of course," he said as enlightenment hit. "The back patio."

They'd spent so much time out there after they'd eaten. Isabella had told him her backyard was her sanctuary. It should've been the first place he looked, especially since the access to the area was through the kitchen, where he'd started his search.

When he reached the door, he stopped, the last thing he needed to do was burst through the doors and startle her.

Confident he had his emotions bottled up enough that they wouldn't explode everywhere, he opened the door. His eyes went to the table where they'd shared so many conversations and there she was. Her shoulders hunched over, a look of defeat in her very posture.

It killed him to know he had done that to her, but their conversation couldn't have been avoided any longer. He'd also known it was a risk embarking on a relationship with her since she'd told him of what happened to her husband, but he'd hoped the get-together at Anna and Zeke's house, not to mention the fact Anna had taken Isabella under her wing, would've shown Isabella she could have what she once wished for, just with him instead.

If his parents lived in Texas, he would've introduced her to them as well, showed her another successful relationship, and how compromise had worked for them. They were currently traveling the world, enjoying his father's retirement and wouldn't be back in the States for another month. In all likelihood, he would miss seeing them, but they were also aware of his deployment date so, if he knew his mom, they'd be back earlier than they'd predicted.

But none of that helped with the situation he was in right now. He had to fix this with Isabella and he had to tell her about his possible promotion.

With measured steps he walked over to where Isabella sat. "Can I join you?"

When she looked up, tears glistened in the sunlight on her cheeks, and a hundred arrows stabbed at his heart. "I don't know if I can do this, Ethan."

Hearing her words, the arrows twisted deeper. He grabbed a chair and scraped it across the concrete until he could sit next to her. Needing to touch her, he reached out and grabbed both of her hands in his. "Talk to me, Izzy, tell me why. Maybe if we can talk we can work this out."

He couldn't lose her, not when he'd found his other half. Telling her he loved her would only make the situation worse, not better.

"I don't know what to say, Ethan, except I'm scared. I'm scared of what could happen to me when you go away. Scared of what could happen to you. What if I'm not strong enough to deal with the separation? I never had to face this with Travis. He was killed before he got deployed."

"Oh, Izzy, you're so much stronger than you think. Do you think for one minute your dad, Meredith, or even Anna and the others, will leave you alone while I'm away? No, you've got a support network here ready and waiting for you."

"I know they'll be there for me. But it won't stop me thinking about all that could go wrong. Worrying about your safety when you walk into buildings where you and Sam are exposed and in danger of bombs and snipers and whatever else lurks around every corner." She pulled her hands from his hold and wrapped them around herself. He wanted to grab them back, maintain their connection.

Now was the time to tell her about his possible promotion; that his days of being a handler were over and he wouldn't be putting himself in immediate danger. "There's something else I need to tell you."

Her head snapped up and fear lurked in her eyes. Man, he hated to see her hurting so much. "What else is there? Isn't you going away in a month to a war zone bad enough?"

Even though she was hurting, he bit back the temptation to snap back that she was well aware of what he did for a living when they first started dating. "A few weeks ago, my commanding officer called me into his office—"

"Wait. What? And you're only telling me this now? Did you get into trouble or something?" Isabella interjected.

"Or something. He spoke to me about a promotion to kennel master. It's a natural progression for me. It's also what they call a STEP promotion."

"What sort of promotion is that? Is it good or bad?"

"A STEP promotion is what they call Stripes for Exceptional Performers."

"So it's a big deal then?"

He sighed and clasped his hands together. "Yeah, it is."

Silence fell between them. A furrow line appeared between Isabella's eyes. She was mulling over everything he told her and he braced himself for what she was going to say or ask next.

"What exactly does a kennel master do? Will you still have to be deployed? Or will you be based stateside permanently?"

Her voice rose in hope as she finished her questions. He could also see a sliver of relief shining in her eyes. God, he hated knowing the second he explained everything he would douse the sparks. "I would be in charge of looking after the dogs. I'd also be responsible for instructing the new recruits that come into the K-9 division. I would no longer be a handler, which means I wouldn't go into any dangerous situations, unless called upon. But, yes, I would still be deployed to oversee the dogs."

Isabella pushed away from the table and walked over to one of the pots filled with roses that dotted a corner of her back patio. Her hand traced the soft petals and he ached to go over to her and hold her in his arms. Tell her everything would be okay. He still had to tell her about his reenlistment. So much he had to heap on her, but he couldn't spread it out no matter how much he wanted to.

What he should've done was tell her when they'd agreed to pursue their relationship after their false starts. But he'd been selfish and had wanted to spend time with Izzy. Even back then, he'd known she was special. She fired emotions in him he'd never experienced before and he didn't want to risk losing that by telling her the truth.

It was a dick move and he was about to pay for his self-ishness.

Sure, back then, it might have ended everything and, yes, it would've hurt but not as much as it would now if she walked away from him. Which he deserved if she did.

"What are you going to do?" she asked.

At least she was still talking to him. "I told him I would think about. There's a lot to consider. Other factors come into play as well."

"What other factors?"

"Well, upon my return, I'll be up for reenlistment."

Her finger tapped against her lip. Without a doubt she was counting back in time, knowing that he knew all of this when they'd agreed to start over for the third time.

"And you've known all of this for over a month."

There was no other option for him; he had to be truthful with her, no matter the consequences. "I wanted to discuss this with you, I really did, but you told me about Travis and, well, the timing never seemed right."

Isabella laughed harshly. "Really? That's such a weak excuse, you know that don't you?"

He stood and began to pace. "You're right it is. I didn't want to tell you because I didn't want to dump the reality of my deployment and everything else onto you all at once. You'd just told me about Travis and things were finally working out with us. I didn't want to hurt you. I just wanted to protect you."

"How is not being truthful protecting me? You have the same flawed logic as my dad when he didn't tell me about Rhonda."

Nothing was going right, as if he ever thought it would. It was always going to be a clusterfuck. "It's not the same at all, Isabella."

"Explain how it's not the same. Certainly seems that way to me. You both decided what was best for me without actually taking my feelings into consideration."

He blew out a frustrated breath. Perhaps he should've said he had been planning to tell her, but he couldn't lie to her. "But I did take your feelings into consideration, Isabella, can't you see that? You told me about your past. We worked through me being away on training exercises. But deployment is different and then there's my promotion and reenlistment." He closed his eyes, ran a hand over his head before opening them to look at her. "I'm sorry, you're right.

I should've spoken to you about everything back then."

"Can I ask you something?"

"What?"

"Putting aside your deployment for the moment, when you got the news about the promotion, what was your immediate thought? The first thing that went through your mind?"

"That it was an honor, but…" He didn't want to voice what had been going through his mind that day.

"But you weren't sure you wanted it because you wouldn't be on the frontlines anymore? You wouldn't be the first one in to protect your team."

Her insight shocked the hell out of him. "Maybe."

"What is the appeal about putting your life in danger every single second of the day? You can't always stop disasters from happening, believe me I know."

Her words cut deep into him, because they were the truth. She would know firsthand about not being able to control everything, but didn't she also understand the honor it was to fight for and protect the country?

"I know that. Do you know what core values of the air force are?"

"No."

"Well, they're *integrity first. Service before self. Excellence in all we do.* I take these very seriously, especially the second one."

"I don't doubt you do, but you also have a God complex,

Ethan, and that's more dangerous than being blasé about what you do. You have to learn to trust others other than yourself." She shook her head and smiled, a sad smile. "I knew I shouldn't have embarked on a relationship with you, Ethan."

A lead balloon filled his stomach. There was no nervousness or apprehension in her voice, just plain conviction. "What are you saying?"

Her fingers fiddled with the sash on her robe, and from where he stood, the rise and fall of her chest wasn't smooth and calm, but rapid and agitated. "I'm saying I don't want to do this anymore. I'm not going to live my life with a man who doesn't believe in me enough to talk about what is happening with his life. I'm sure you've already made the decision to reenlist, haven't you?"

He nodded, the words impossibly lodged behind a large lump of disgust in this throat.

"I would never have asked you to choose between me and your career. I don't have that right, considering the newness of our relationship. But we could've still discussed it all, Ethan. To grow as a couple, we have to know what is happening in each other's lives. I'm not going to go through my life with a man who hides an integral part of who he is out of a misguided need to protect. I want you to leave, Ethan."

Damn, how had everything gone wrong so quickly? Weren't they having the type of discussion she just said she wanted?

Yes and no. He'd made decisions without talking to her. Decisions that affected their potential future. He'd pounded the nails into his own coffin.

"Is that what you want? There's nothing I can say to change your mind? No amount of apology to make it better?"

"Oh, Ethan, if only it were that simple. But I fear this is going to be a pattern. And, to be truthful, I don't think I can handle you being deployed, even with your promotion and you not being on the frontline. It was hard enough to get over Travis. Having to do it again? I've got a choice and I've made it."

The finality of her tone cut deep. He'd hoped that somehow she would be willing to take another chance. He'd been creating dreams when he shouldn't have been.

Irrational anger flared to life. "Well, then, I hope you have a nice life in your safe little world, because the reason you can live in your world is because of me and my friends and our passion to keep this country safe."

He strode past her, ignoring the tears streaming down her cheeks. She'd made her decision. The fact his heart was crumbling in a million pieces didn't matter to her, because she had no idea how he felt. Now he was glad he'd kept his true feelings hidden.

A broken heart would heal.

Chapter Sixteen

THE FINAL BELL for the year rang and the kids jumped up cheering. Isabella forced a smile she wasn't feeling onto her face.

"Have a wonderful summer, kids. Be careful and don't forget to read some of the suggested reading material. I'm going to miss you and you're going to do a fantastic job in middle school."

The kids rushed up to her and gave her quick hugs before running out the door, their laughter filling the hallways. Normally, her heart would be bursting with pride watching her kids move into the next phase of their lives, but this year, it was like she was watching from the outside looking in.

She sat back down and looked around her empty classroom. During the last couple of days they'd all worked together to take down the various posters and work that had been hung up on the walls during the school year. The room resembled a barren shell, like her insides. Ever since she'd told Ethan to leave, she'd been desolate and alone. More than she ever thought she would be.

"Stop it," she said out loud to the empty classroom. "You

made your decision and it's the right one. Now it's time to enjoy your summer and come August, you'll be ready to tackle a new lot of fifth graders."

Yeah, saying it out loud didn't make a lick of difference to how she was feeling. She had an idea nothing would.

"You ready to escape this gin joint?" Meredith's perky voice broke into her morose introspection.

"Yep, pity we have to come back next week to finalize everything."

Meredith plonked herself down in her usual place opposite Isabella's desk. "True, but then it's ten weeks of sheer, unadulterated bliss of doing nothing but sleeping, binge watching the shows I couldn't watch all school year and sleeping."

"You mentioned sleeping twice," Isabella responded drily.

"Deliberately, you look like shit, Iz. How much sleep have you gotten over the last couple of weeks?"

Meredith had answered her tearful call that Saturday and had come over bearing wine and cheese. She'd listened to Isabella spill all the details about the conversation with Ethan and the evening before with her dad. Being the good friend that she was, Meredith had listened and hadn't passed judgment. Somehow, her friend's leniency had passed and now Meredith was going to tell her exactly how it was.

"I've slept enough."

"Bullshit, Iz, you miss him. It's obvious in the way you

pretend to not constantly check your phone to see if you've got a message at lunchtime. It's in the way you smile but it isn't your usual Isabella smile. The kids have been so excited about the end of the school year that they had no idea this Ms. Knowles was completely different to the Ms. Knowles of a month ago. Love and happiness shone out of you, it was quite sickening if you ask me."

"I was not in love," Isabella protested, but it was a lie and she knew the second the words left her mouth.

"Right, and that's why a little red star isn't marked on next Wednesday's date on your wall calendar."

Crap, she thought she'd done it small enough that no one would notice. Of course, Meredith had. In a low point of pity, she'd made a note of his departure date. Sleep had been terrible because every time she'd fallen asleep she'd been pummeled with dreams of him and Sam entering a building and the building blowing up. Or Ethan reaching out to her and she was unable to grab hold of him before he disappeared into a black abyss.

It was getting to the stage where she was afraid to close her eyes. Afraid to see what other tragedy her brain could come up with. She wanted the dreams she'd had before their breakup. Dreams of them living in her house, a little girl running around the backyard being chased by Sam while Ethan stood by the grill flipping burgers while she nursed a newborn baby.

Dreams she hadn't admitted to herself how much she

wanted them to come true.

"Enough," she said out loud shocking herself and Meredith.

"Enough what, Iz?"

"Wallowing in self-pity. Summer's coming and I'm going to enjoy every minute of it." Maybe if she told herself enough times that was what she was going to do, it might actually come true.

"Are you going to see Ethan before he leaves?" Meredith asked quietly.

Isabella's heart folded in on itself at the mention of his name. "No, Mere, I'm not. It's over, and it would never have worked. It's better this way."

"Oh, so you don't think breaking his heart before he leaves to go to a war zone isn't going to be on his mind and distract him?"

Isabella shook her head, not wanting to believe he was hurting as much as she was. "Don't say that, Meredith."

"Why not? I'm sure it's the truth." Her friend got up and stopped beside her, wrapping an arm around Isabella. "I saw the way he looked at you, Iz. He worshipped every step you took. His face lit up the second he laid eyes on you. Are you sure there's no way you two can be together?"

It wasn't the first time she'd been asked that question. Much to her surprise, Anna had reached out to her and they'd met up for a coffee. Isabella had cuddled her baby and they'd talked. She would tell Meredith exactly what she told

Anna.

"No, Mere. I just know I can't live my life in constant fear that something will happen to him."

"I thought you worked through this months ago. You can't live this way. Fear shouldn't hold you back. When you were with him you were happier than I've ever seen you. Why would you throw it all away?"

"It's not just him being away. It's because he didn't trust me enough to talk about our future."

"Oh please, so he didn't tell you about his promotion straightaway or the fact he was going to reenlist. You'd just started dating. Those types of discussions don't happen after you've been dating a week. It takes time to build up to them. But at least he told you." Meredith stood. "You grasped at a lame reason to break up with him because you're still living in fear. But the question is, has it made you happy?"

Isabella let the truth of her friend's words sink in. It was a question she didn't want to answer, because if she were truthful with herself, she was more miserable than she'd ever been.

She'd made a huge mistake.

FOUR HOURS LATER Isabella stood at her father's doorstep wondering why she was here and not at home.

Once she'd left school it had been automatic to head

home, but that was the last place she wanted to be. Too many memories of Ethan lurked around every corner. So she'd kept driving and somehow her subconscious had led her to her dad's doorstep.

Why was she here?

She and her dad never had the sort of relationship where she shared her burdens with him. They were in a rebuilding phase at the moment, but there was still a lot of ground to cover.

With a sigh of exasperation, she turned to leave but the door opened at that exact moment.

"Honey bee, why are you leaving? You didn't even knock."

Her eyes drifted shut hearing the censure in his tone. Yet another person she'd disappointed.

Turning back around, she walked up to her dad and wrapped her arms around him, laying her head on his chest, inhaling the reassuring scent of Old Spice. After half a heartbeat, his arms closed around her holding her tightly. He took a couple of steps backward and she followed until they were inside his house. She registered the door slamming shut, but was conscious only of the movement of her dad's hand up and down her spine, comforting her when she needed it the most.

"Isabella, what's wrong?"

"I messed everything up, Dad. I may have ruined the best thing in my life and I don't know how to fix it."

"Are you talking about Ethan?" he asked, and she could only respond with a nod. "Come on, honey bee, let's sit down."

With an arm securely around her, her father steered her into the living room, settling her on the couch before sitting beside her, taking one of her hands in his.

"I'm sure it's not as bad as you're thinking. Why don't you tell me what's going on?" Her father's voice was low and measured and comforting all at the same time.

"It's so stupid now that I look back on it. I got mad at him for not trusting me enough to tell me about the promotion he'd been offered. His upcoming deployment and the fact he's due to reenlist soon. It happened the morning after you and Rhonda came over for dinner."

"Ahh, I know I've already said I'm sorry about that, but I truly am. I was being selfish in wanting to keep you to myself while we rebuilt our relationship. You shared Ethan with me and I should've given you the same courtesy."

"It's okay, Dad, I do understand… now."

"I know Ethan getting deployed scares you. That your mind drifts to what happened to Travis. But the situations couldn't be more different. Ethan and his squadron are trained for all situations. Every single man will look out for his brothers-in-arms."

"I know, Dad. But they can't stop a missile attack while in a convoy. Or stepping on a hidden land mine while they're patrolling. I just don't know if I can cope with not knowing how he is every minute he's apart from me."

"And he could be in a car accident or get sick while state-side. Nothing in life is guaranteed, Isabella, you of all people know that." Her father sighed beside her. "Do you want to know why I set you up on a date with Ethan, knowing he was in the military?"

"Why?"

"Because when you were enmeshed in military life all those years ago, joy radiated out of you. I wanted you to be that happy again. And you were. The times I saw you with Ethan, you were my happy girl again. The one who couldn't wait to be a military wife. I don't know if you and Ethan had ever talked about the future, and I'm not an expert on relationships, but the connection between the two of you was visible. You could almost touch it. Rhonda commented on it too." Her father took her hand and squeezed. "It was tragic when Travis died, but you're young and it's okay to live your life. You shouldn't give up."

"I know. Meredith and I talked about it. I was ready to grasp life with both hands, but when it came to it, I can't push myself over the edge."

"I just think you don't want to. I want to ask you something."

Meredith had asked this same question. "If you're going to ask me if I'm happy, don't bother."

"I can see the answer to that question myself. My question is different."

"Okay, what is it?"

"If the phone rang right this second and it was someone telling you that Ethan had been hurt, what would you do? How would you feel?"

Isabella's stomach dropped and she clutched her arms around herself. "How could you say that to me, Dad? You know that's my biggest fear. I would never recover if something happened to Ethan. It would be worse than what I went through with Travis."

"Why, honey bee? Why would it be worse?"

The time had come to truly accept what she'd been trying so hard to ignore. She pushed down the sense of betrayal. "Because I love him more than I ever loved Travis. And I don't want spend the rest of my life the way I've been living it the last couple of weeks."

"And how is that, Isabella?"

"I've been so miserable. I'd rather have him for a short while than not at all."

Her dad's hands landed on her shoulders and he turned her. She looked up and another batch of tears welled up in her eyes when she recognized the love shining out of her father's eyes. A look he'd always had when he looked at her but she had been too stubborn to see.

"You have your answer right there, honey bee. I have no doubt you're feeling guilty about the depth of your love for Ethan in comparison to Travis, but don't. Travis would be happy for you, you know that."

"I hope you're right."

"I know I am. All that matters now is that you've admitted to yourself you love Ethan, and I have no doubt he loves you. I saw it in action that night at your place. His unconditional support of you told me everything I needed to know. He's a good man and he's the perfect man for you. I watched him as he followed your every move that night. The way he always touched you. If I know military men, and I think I do, he will do everything in his power to be extra vigilant and come back to you every time he's deployed. You have to trust him and trust in the love you have for him and the love he has for you."

She wanted to grasp onto her father's words tightly. Everyone kept saying that Ethan loved her, but he'd never spoken the words to her. Then again, she hadn't spoken the words to him.

The time had come to trust herself, trust her love for Ethan, and take that leap, because the mere thought of losing Ethan and then having another man touch her or kiss her sent shivers of revulsion through her.

Ethan was it for her.

She'd known it the second she watched him walk away from her that day in her garden, but she'd been too afraid to chase after him and admit her mistake.

The question was how did Ethan feel about her?

DEPLOYMENT DAY ROLLED around bright and sunny and yet, Ethan felt cold and dreary inside. He'd been feeling this way since he and Isabella had broken up. What he needed to do was push the thought away, he couldn't go away this distracted, too many people depended on him.

Yet he still scanned the crowd of family members milling around to see everyone off. Zeke, Anna, and their baby were wrapped up in each other's arms. As well as many of the other guys.

His parents had always come to see him off and he'd taken their presence for granted he now realized. He'd spoken to them on the phone this morning, they'd told him they were going to be there, but a plane delay had meant they wouldn't get back in time. He'd told them it was fine, but now he wished they were here.

"Hi, Ethan."

Everything in him froze and he was sure his heart had stopped beating. Had he imagined Isabella's voice? He had to have. She hadn't made any attempt to contact him since that day in her backyard.

Even though it had killed him, he'd respected her wishes and hadn't called or texted her no matter how many times he'd wanted to pick up the phone and do that or get in his car and drive to her place.

Turning slowly, sure he was going to be disappointed and find Izzy wasn't there, his eyes collided with a beautiful pair of blue ones. The same eyes that had haunted his sleep every singled night.

"Isabella?"

The vision in front of him nodded and he didn't think; just acted. Grabbing her tightly in a hug, he relished the scent of her perfume.

"I'm sorry," she whispered over and over in his ear. "I'm sorry for hurting you."

He pulled back and looked down at her, wiping away the single tear trickling down her cheek. "I'm sorry too. I knew about your past and how it's shaped you. I shouldn't have kept my promotion and reenlistment orders from you." He framed her face with his hands, needing to let her know how he felt. If she didn't return his feelings that was fine, but her being here had to mean she at least cared for him. "I love you, Isabella Knowles. I know there's a lot we still need to work out, but I love you and I can't imagine not having you in my life. The last few weeks have been horrible. I know we can do anything together."

The tears flowed freely down her cheeks but her smile pierced him straight in the heart. It wasn't a smile of fear, it was a smile full of hope.

"I love you too, Ethan. I couldn't let you leave without telling you. I've been so miserable too without you these last fe—"

Ethan stopped the flow of her words with his lips. She loved him and that was all that mattered to him. The rest could be sorted out, but he needed this physical connection to convey everything he was feeling for her. Her mouth opened up under his, allowing him to deepen the kiss. Their tongues tangled and he pulled her tighter against him, never wanting to let her go.

The sound of catcalls and whistles penetrated his desire-laden consciousness and he reluctantly pulled away from her. He looked up and saw the members of his squadron and their partners clapping at him and Isabella.

"Oh, my God, I created a scene, didn't I?" she said, her cheeks a beautiful shade of pink.

"The best kind," he responded. "Although your timing could've been better. I think I'm going to spend the whole of my deployment in a state of arousal now."

The blush deepened in her cheeks, but she laughed. "We'll just have to work something out." Her faced turned serious. "I want you to know I'm committed to you, Ethan. I know there will be times when I freak out, but I also know that I'm not alone and more importantly, you aren't alone out there."

"I have no doubt we'll work it out because I'm never letting you go again, Izzy. I love you. You're it for me."

"I love you too. And you're it for me as well."

He was about to lean down and kiss her again when the call came for them all to board the plane. "I've got to go, Izzy."

For a split second, fear entered her eyes before it was replaced by an inner determination he'd never seen before. "I know. Go and do your job. Just come home, okay?"

"Always," he whispered against her lips.

Epilogue

FINALLY, AFTER SIX long months, she'd be able to see and hold Ethan. Erratic Skype calls just weren't the same as being about to reach out and touch his face.

She rubbed her hand over her belly. That had been the hardest secret of all to keep. She was pregnant. Had found out a month after he'd left.

To say she was shocked was an understatement. It seemed that last morning at her house before their breakup they'd had a condom failure and as a result she and Ethan were about to become parents way earlier than they'd planned.

During their talks, they'd sorted out a lot of their relationship and were committed to each other. It had taken everything in her not to blurt out her news when they'd been talking, but she wanted to surprise him.

She had no doubt he wouldn't have any concerns about the paternity of the baby. She'd found out Ethan and her father had been in touch during their short breakup. Ethan had wanted to make sure she was okay and her father, the sneaky man that he was, had kept it from her. This time she didn't get upset because it warmed her heart to know she had two men who cared for her.

"Are you ready?" Anna asked as she stepped up beside her, holding her baby who was now seven months old and sported one bottom tooth. Zeke was going to be surprised when he saw how big his son was now.

During the time Ethan had been away, she and Anna had gotten close. Meredith had been offered a once-in-a-lifetime opportunity to teach overseas, and so her best friend had jumped at it. By the time she returned, Isabella would have the baby in her arms.

Meredith was her best friend, but Anna had helped her during the early stages of her pregnancy and had recommended her doctor.

"Yep. I'm ready." She answered Anna with a big smile.

"You know there's a bet going on among the girls that Ethan's going to pass out when he sees you're pregnant."

Isabella laughed and her baby kicked in response. She didn't know what the sex of their child was, she wanted to find out with Ethan, which was why she'd made an appointment for the next day, to have another ultrasound so Ethan could see his baby and they could find out the sex together.

"Here they are."

The big military transport wheels hit the tarmac with a screech and a plume of smoke. Isabella released her breath. Her man was home safe and sound, just like he said he would be.

Ten minutes later the plane's back hatch lowered and she got a glimpse of the men all eager to exit.

She shielded her eyes and as they got closer she was able to pick out Ethan easily. Unlike all the other women around her who were running toward their men, Isabella could only walk slowly. The downside of being almost eight months pregnant.

The second Ethan's eyes landed on hers his duffel dropped to the ground and his mouth hung open. Oh God, what if he thought he wasn't the father? No matter how sure she was that he wouldn't question her, at that very moment, the doubts crowded in.

She shouldn't have been worried because Ethan forgot his bag and sprinted toward her.

"We're pregnant?" he asked, but didn't wait for a response, he just grabbed her tight and crashed his lips down on hers.

Happy tears flowed down her cheeks, mingling with their kiss. Not happy about being squashed between the two of them the baby kicked. Ethan sprang back and looked down at her protruding belly.

"Surprise," she said.

His hands went to touch her belly, but stopped before connecting. "Can I?" Uncertainty filled his eyes and that was the last thing she wanted to see.

Taking a deep breath she took a step, closing the gap between his hands and her belly, then laid her own over his. "Say hello to your son or daughter."

Her breath hitched when he bent down and placed a soft kiss on her belly. "Hey, baby, I'm your daddy."

The tears returned at hearing the conviction in his voice when he said the word *daddy*. But she still couldn't quite get rid of the worry. "Did I do the right thing by not telling you?"

"Oh, Izzy, you did. This is the best surprise ever. I love you and…" He dropped down on one knee and pulled a box out of his pocket. "This is what I was going to do the minute I saw you. I love you more than life itself Isabella Knowles. You make me a better man and I want to spend the rest of my life with you. Will you marry me?"

Her eyes popped at the diamond ring sitting snugly in red velvet. The ring was stunning in its simplicity. She had no idea how he was able to get such a beautiful ring while he was deployed but there was never any doubt to her answer. "Yes, Ethan, I will marry you."

His smile grew even wider than it was as he stood and slipped the ring on her finger. "A perfect fit just like us."

She sighed as his arms came around her and his head lowered toward hers. "Yes, we are a perfect fit."

The End

Acknowledgements

I'm thrilled to be part of the Tule family and can't thank them enough for their belief in my storytelling abilities and support they've given me. A huge thank you to Julie, my editor, for wrangling this book into the shape it is. What a journey that was.

Sometimes you meet someone and you just click. That person for me is my writing partner and best friend Abigail Owen. Since April 2016 she has been a staple in my writing life and I couldn't have got half the words and stories written that I have without her and our sprinting sessions. Her support means the world to me. Love you, girl!

Jennifer, my tireless PA, thanks for doing all the other stuff that needs to be done when you're an author and leaving me free to write my words.

To Shey and Shawn for answering my endless text messages about all things air force. I hope I got everything right. Any errors within the text are my own.

To my family, as always, I can't do half the stuff I do without knowing that I have your love pushing me to keep going.

The Man's Best Friend series

Book 1: *Blind Date Bet*

Book 2: *Next Door Knight*

Book 3: Coming Soon

Available now at your favorite online retailer!

About the Author

USA Today Bestselling author Nicole Flockton writes sexy contemporary romances, seducing you one kiss at a time as you turn the pages. Nicole likes nothing better than taking characters and creating unique situations where they fight to find their true love.

On her first school report her teacher noted "Nicole likes to tell her own stories". It wasn't until after the birth of her first child and after having fun on a romance community forum that she finally decided to take the plunge and write a book. Now with over 20 books published she hasn't looked back.

Apart from writing Nicole is busy looking after her very own hero – her wonderfully supportive husband, and two fabulous kids. She also enjoys watching sports and, of course, reading.

You can visit Nicole at her website www.nicoleflockton.com or follow her on twitter at twitter.com/NicoleFlockton

Thank you for reading

Blind Date Bet

If you enjoyed this book, you can find more from all our great authors at TulePublishing.com, or from your favorite online retailer.

TULE
PUBLISHING

Made in the USA
Las Vegas, NV
19 May 2023